CRISIS IN GREENVILLE

A Novel About a Threatened Baseball Stadium and a Team of Rejects

By JOE R. BLAKELY

Other books by Joe R. Blakely

Lifting Oregon Out of the Mud
Building the Oregon Coast Highway

A Tribute to McArthur Court, 1891-1932

The Bellfountain Giant Killers
A miraculous 1937 state high school basketball championship

Eugene's Civic Stadium
From muddy football games to professional baseball

The Tall Firs
1939: The First NCAA Basketball Champions

NOVELS

Kidnapped
On Oregon's Coast Highway (1926)

The Heirloom
Bandon, Oregon (1921)

CRISIS IN GREENVILLE

Joe R. Blakely

Author of *Eugene's Civic Stadium*

CraneDance Publications
Eugene, OR

Crisis in Greenville

A Novel About a Threatened Baseball Stadium
and a Team of Rejects

PUBLISHED BY CRANEDANCE PUBLICATIONS
PO Box 50535, Eugene OR 97405
(541) 345-3974 • www.cranedance.com

November 2010

ISBN: ISBN 978-0-9824441-5-3

Printed in the United States of America

PRINTING HISTORY
First edition: November 2010

Author Contact:
541-688-4643 • josephb@uoregon.edu

I wish to dedicate this book to all the people who spent time, money, and effort in trying to save Eugene Oregon's Civic Stadium.

Acknowledgments

The idea for this story came to me while researching the 1974 Eugene Emeralds' baseball team. They were a team of rejects, and *special*. Their true story is told in my book *Eugene's Civic Stadium*. My fiction story, *Crisis in Greenville,* uses that theme—a team of rejects is assembled in a short period of time to play in a professional baseball league.

I wish to thank these people: Saundra Miles, Martha Bayless, Rebecca Morales, Mabel Armstrong, Wayne Harrison, William Sullivan, Rachael Wolfgang, and Marvin L. Van Wyck, who helped to make this novel possible.

Special thanks go to Barbara and Dan Gleason for helping me publish my work; for the formatting, covers, and additional creative editing.

But most of all I wish to thank William Sullivan, who did the final editing. He is a newspaper columnist and author of numerous Oregon hiking books, plus has written books on Oregon history, and entertaining novels.

Chapter One

"Thank God!" Marge said angrily. "At last we're rid of that baseball team and their obnoxious fans." Her coffee mug hit the end table with a thud, splashing coffee on magazines. That morning's May 1st, 1974 issue of the *Greenville News* rested in her lap. The headline: "GIANTS LEAVE TOWN."

With her red bathrobe, yellow scarf, and white face-cream she could have passed as a carnival clown. Yet in the town of Greenville she was no clown—she was attractive, intelligent, and highly respected. She was a competitor, a fighter. People who opposed her usually lost. That's why the stadium was such a big issue to her. She hadn't gotten her way, yet.

She took a deep drag on her cigarette and thought. With the Giants gone the stadium would be up for grabs. Marge knew what she'd do with it—she'd blow it to smithereens, and with good reason: the noise, the litter, the bright lights and heavy traffic. It all affected her quality of life, and she wasn't the only one. The stadium was only three blocks from her house.

As she exhaled, smoke plumed. She carefully snuffed out the cigarette in the ashtray. At 62 she was wealthy. She and her husband had made many wise investments. "If only we owned that stadium we could put that land to good use," she said aloud.

Marge picked up her mug and sipped. She looked up at Arthur's aging face and bristly grey hair. Though stooped with age he was still about six-feet-six inches tall. Wrapped around his thin frame was a brown robe. He stood at the front window looking down on the roof of the Giants' stadium, at the foot of University Hill. Marge saw him look to the east into the sun's scorching light. He turned from the glare and looked down at her.

"We need to pounce on this opportunity. Everyone says a stadium like that simply doesn't fit into a neighborhood like ours." Arthur carefully tested his hot coffee. "Now that the Giants are gone maybe the city council will listen to reason. I want to buy that property, Marge. We could triple our investment. All we'd have to do is get the city council to change the zoning to commercial."

"I wouldn't count on our city council doing anything wise," Marge said. The doorbell rang. "Who could that be?"

"Probably Ridley. He knows I want the stadium. He'd be a good partner."

Arthur shuffled through the hall to the front door. The door creaked as it swung open. In rushed Ridley along with a fresh breeze. He was rosy cheeked, and stout as a brick. He came into the front room and sat on a cushioned chair facing Marge. Marge frantically wiped cream from her face and quickly removed curlers. Ridley was twenty years younger than Arthur and a foot shorter. He had a thick crop of unruly black hair. Marge thought it looked good on him.

"Did you read the paper?" Ridley asked.

"Yes," Arthur said. Marge moved over so Arthur could sit next to her. Marge pulled out her diamond-studded gold cigarette lighter and clicked the flint. The spark blazed to life on the wick. She watched the fire bobbing for a second, then sucked in, igniting her cigarette. The lighter had been a present from Arthur on their fortieth anniversary. A special inscription read, "To Marge: Thanks for forty wonderful years. Love, Arthur." Even though Marge had few friends, one person had stolen her heart and that was Arthur. The morning sun flared behind Ridley.

"Pull the shade down, would you, Ridley?" Marge asked as she exhaled.

Ridley pulled on the dangling cord and the morning light snapped off. He returned to his chair. Ridley leaned forward.

"Now's the time to confront the city council. We need to convince them to sell the property. After all, the city has been hoping to raise taxes. They need money. We'll give it to them. In exchange, we'd get a nice chunk of commercial property. Everyone's happy."

"Not the baseball fans," Marge said.

"They're a minority," Ridley scoffed. "The professional baseball season starts next month. No one could form a new team in that amount of time. The lumber barons who built the stadium forty years ago are long dead. It's 1974, Marge. Lumber mills are not as profitable as they once were, and baseball is losing its popularity."

"There's more to it than that, Ridley," Marge said, letting out a whiff of smoke. "Listen, I want that damned stadium outta here too, but there are some people who are fond of it. It's got history, and they'll try to find a new team. Those are the people we'll have to fight."

"Nonsense," Ridley countered. "Baseball fans are the poorest residents in Greenville. They don't have the cash to buy a new team. With no team the stadium will have to be sold."

"I think you're right, Ridley," Arthur said, combing his gray hair back. "The only person that could stop us is that S.O.B. Jack Mayfield. But with the mayor on our side we may have a majority on the council. Let's get to work. The city council meets tomorrow night."

Chapter Two

At 28, Jack Mayfield was the youngest person ever to represent zone 6 on the city council. He had black curly hair and a lean build. He loved to watch baseball games. Since a child, when his father took him to the games, he'd followed the Giants' seasons—their winning years and losing years. Still, they'd never won a pennant. He hoped that some year they would, and that he'd be there to see it. For the last 41 years either a semi-pro or professional baseball team had used the stadium.

He and his best friend, Burt Andrews, a former catcher in the Pacific Coast League and town hero, would talk about the game of baseball for hours. Both thought the game and the stadium were sacred.

"Our stadium is the best little stadium in the country," Burt said.

"My grandfather," Jack said, "organized the entire town to build it."

"I wonder what it was like in the 40s when they had the semi-pro lumbermen's league playing here?" Burt asked.

"Granddad told me it was the biggest happening in town. Like gladiator contests during the Roman Empire. Spectators would flock here to see the teams compete. They didn't have television so they came to the stadium for their entertainment. The outstanding players were town heroes.

"The players came from local lumber mills, factories, and other businesses. During the summer months they'd get off work, then rush to the stadium to practice. Those guys were probably dead tired from their jobs, yet they loved the game."

"Were they paid?" Burt asked.

"Yes, and to some it was like a second job. But a job that was fun. Granddad said the players looked forward to the next Sunday and the hallowed game. They awarded pennants just like the major leagues. Along with the crowds came the players' girl friends. The players dreamed about making it to the major leagues. A few did. Local sportswriters followed their careers. They were like Greenville gods. Oh, granddad said those weekly games where so exciting."

"I wish I could have seen just one game," Burt said.

"I know which game I'd like to have seen," Jack said. "1940, here in our stadium, the greatest black pitcher of all time, Satchel Paige, pitched against the best talent the lumbermen's league could put together. He came with the Kansas City Monarchs, an all-black team from Back East. Once their season ended they headed out west to barnstorm up the west coast. Every year in the early 40s the Monarchs came, like migratory birds.

"My granddad said it wasn't much different here than down south—the black man was treated with contempt and racial bias. They had to sleep in their bus. Satchel, who drove a big Cadillac, was granted the right to park his car inside the cyclone fence, next to the ball field. Then when the game started, Satchel would bring the crowd to their feet laughing with his patter, like a jester in a king's court. Granddad said Satchel would have his team sit down on the field. Then he'd strike out the batters as easy as eating apple pie. The amazing thing was that the people were so enthralled and excited about watching Satchel they forgot the team was black. But after the game, as night darkened the prejudice returned. The Monarchs would go back to their bus and Satchel to his Cadillac."

With Jack's love of baseball it was hardly likely that he'd

tolerate an attack on the old stadium. Yet, he really didn't see the attack coming. Mayfield was a real estate broker with eight sales representatives working for him. His sales manager, Robert Moore, handled most of the day-to-day operations. This gave Jack time to run for public office and help with the business of the city. Mayfield had many reasons to be happy. He'd won an elective office, he ran a successful business, and he had a nice home in the University neighborhood. Women admired him, and he had many good friends.

Jack first suspected trouble on the morning of May 1st when his secretary Sally Bolling brought him that morning's copy of the *Greenville News*. Jack's six-foot frame reclined back in his swivel desk chair, his feet propped on the desk. Just as Sally went out the door Jack's feet crashed to the floor. He stared at the news story in disbelief. The Greenville Giants had left town for a bigger city in California. The Greenville Giants had morphed into the Sacramental Bees. Wealthy investors had already approached Tom Brand, Greenville's city mayor, about purchasing the stadium. "Not if I have anything to say about it," Jack said, slamming the newspaper on his desk.

Jack knew what the investors would do. They'd tear the stadium down and build condominiums, business offices, and shopping malls. Surely the game of baseball and the preservation of the stadium outweighed a commercial development. As an elected representative, he intended to let the city council know just how he felt tomorrow night.

Chapter 3

Overhead fluorescent lights illuminated the semi-circular room. The chamber resembled an amphitheater, with the seats rising towards the back. Noisy citizens filled the seats and more stood at the back. The councilors sat at a long table in the front. Jack Mayfield sat to the far left. He looked out at the sea of faces. He represented townspeople in zone 6. The other councilors represented the remaining five zones. Jack's zone included University Hill and the stadium. Mayor Tom Brand sat in the middle and could vote only in case of a tie. Jack noticed Ridley whispering something to Arthur and Marge. They sat in the front row. Sitting next to them was an attractive woman taking notes.

"Who's that?" Jack asked Susan Byrd, the plump blond councilor from zone 5 sitting to his left.

"That's Anne Richards. She's from southern California. San Diego, I think. She's been here about two years. She just landed the job as sports writer for the Greenville News."

"How did a woman land that job?"

"I've heard she's really gutsy."

"She'd have to be. Is she married?"

"No, but rumors ..."

"Quiet!" Brand tapped his gavel on the table. "This meeting is called to order. We're here to discuss the future of Greenville's stadium. I'd like to encourage audience participation. The question confronting us is this: The Greenville Giants have left town. They've gone to California and have taken a new name, the Sacramento Bees. Our stadium lies empty. What are we going to do with the stadium and its 10-acre plot of land? Every speaker will have exactly five minutes, and not a second longer. If that is understood, let's begin." Tom snuffed his cigarette into the ashtray.

A man advanced to speak at the podium. "My name is Sam Bacon, I live in zone 3. I'm the curator for our museum. As you all know, our stadium is not only a baseball field, but a historical treasure. In the early 1930s, the citizens of Greenville voted to build our stadium. Councilors, it's the building that concerns me. Our stadium is one of five of this type still standing in the country. Our local paper has written an editorial advocating tearing the stadium down. How on earth can we think like that? It's a shrine! Please, don't tear it down." Jack smiled as the crowd erupted in applause, whistles, and shouts.

"Come to order!" Mayor Brand said. "There will be no more outbursts like that. Applause is not needed in these chambers. Boos and hurrahs will be cause for eviction, is that clear? Next speaker, please."

"My name is Burt Andrews from zone 2. I represent a group of 250 citizens that has recently formed to save the stadium. We agree with Sam that the stadium is an important historical treasure. We think the city should look for another Greenville Giant team. Our group is looking, too. I have some connections, and just might be able to put together a team in time for this season. We need to keep a professional baseball team in this town. Baseball games represent family entertainment at an affordable cost. We have a fabulous stadium, so let's use it!"

As Burt sat down, Ridley approached the microphone. "My name is Jason Ridley, and I represent a group of investors that would like to develop the 10 acres in question." The crowd hushed. "It's not our intention to dishonor the stadium. But the stadium rests on valuable land. It should be earning tax dollars. With these funds the city could fix roads, pay for schools, and rebuild outdated municipal buildings. If the stadium is going to sit there unoccupied, then it ought to be demolished. The way it stands now, the city of Greenville has a money-eating monstrosity on its hands. As city councilors, it's up to you to keep the city's best interests in mind. Sometimes your decisions may not be popular. We should work together and replace that old dilapidated structure with buildings that produce strong tax revenue. Thank you."

Amid the whispers started by Ridley's presentation, a small girl walked down the aisle towards the microphone.

"My name is Tracie Andrews from zone 2; I'm a sixth grader at Greenville Elementary. I have a petition signed by 25 students who want to keep the stadium. For the last two years, I've really, really enjoyed watching baseball games. It's a fun place to be and I like meeting my friends there. Please don't tear it down." She walked up to the councilors' table and put down her petition.

Marge Beckley, in a light colored paisley dress, moved to the microphone. Jack knew she hated the stadium.

Her delicate, trim physique gently shook while she spoke. "I have a petition signed by 45 University Hill taxpaying residents. We hope you'll decide to do away with professional baseball in zone 6. On game nights the bright field lights keep us up late, and the noise is so bad we can't even hear our televisions." As she gained her composure, her reedy voice crackled over the PA system. "The next day we're forced to clean up the beer bottles and cigarette packages. Some nights the parking is so bad the fans use our driveways. We have reached the end of our patience." Then Marge moved closer to the microphone. Her green eyes blazed as she whispered, "Councilors, tear down that stadium!" She finished her presentation by handing her petition to the mayor.

Jack listened to the pros and cons of the following speakers. The stadium's supporters far outnumbered the stadium's opponents. But Jack knew where he stood. His father had always said "Son, that stadium saved this community during the 1930s. It was Greenville's biggest WPA project. That stadium represents the sweat and tears of this community."

Jack knew he must save the stadium and form another Greenville Giants baseball team.

When the last speaker walked from the microphone, the public session came to an end. The people filed out of the chambers, leaving the councilors to make a decision. Jack listened for another hour as the councilors debated the matter. The councilors were seriously considering selling the property.

"Enough discussion," Tom declared and pounded his gavel on the table.

At that moment Jack knew he had to gamble the stadium's fate in order to save it.

"Does anyone want to make a motion?" Tom said.

"Yes" Jack said. "I move that we try and find another baseball team. If we haven't found one in a month then we sell the property."

"Is there a second to the motion?" Tom asked.

"Yes," George Putman said.

"All in favor of the motion raise your hands," Tom said. The councilors from zones 1 and 2 were against, but the rest agreed.

"The motion carries." Tom said. "Jack, you have 30 days to find a team. If you fail, the stadium will be sold to the highest bidder."

Chapter 4

Burt Andrews greeted Jack as he came outside. "Hey, what about my daughter Tracie?"

"Very poised for a sixth grader, tell her good job."

"I will. What happened in there anyway, Jack?"

"We've 30 days to get a berth in a baseball league and put together a team."

"Jesus, it can't be done!" Burt said.

"We have to, and it must be done before June 2nd. It's our last chance to save the stadium and professional baseball in Greenville."

"I've heard that the Pacific North League's owners are meeting in Portland tomorrow," Burt said. "There's a vacancy and they need another team for the eight-member league. I don't know if they'd be interested in an independent team. If you can get us a berth, I may be able to put a team together."

"We've got to try," Jack said. "We have our sports business organization already in place, the investors from the old Giants team. I'm positive they'll support a new Greenville team. I need to meet with the Pacific North League owners tomorrow. That means I'll have to drive to Portland tonight. I know a few of them and they might give me an audience. In the meantime, you start rounding up those players. If I'm successful we'll need every eligible baseball player we can find. Burt, with you as manager and my connections we just might pull this miracle off."

Anne Richards confronted Jack next. She stood just five feet tall. A cool breeze rustled her short brown hair. She wore a white blouse and a dark patterned skirt. She waved a pad and pencil in the air.

"I'm a reporter for the *Greenville News*."

"So I'm told."

"I need to ask you some questions," Anne said. Suddenly Susan Byrd came rushing out of the chamber doors. She bumped into Anne, sending her pencil and pad flying.

"I'm terribly sorry!" Susan cried. Susan bent her plump body down, picking up the pad with some effort. The pencil kept rolling down the steps. Jack and Anne descended after the pencil. Near the bottom step they collided. Anne fell across the sidewalk and onto the blacktop of the busy street. Jack scrambled after her, as cars honked and tires squealed. He plucked her up and carried her quickly back to the safety of the sidewalk. She didn't weigh much, and seemed all right. Jack was a little sorry he'd have to set her down, but he did so apologizing profusely. The smell of perfume lingered. Susan caught up with them and gave the pad to Anne.

"Gosh, I'm sorry. Are you all right?"

"A little scraped up, but I'm fine."

"I'm off to another meeting," Susan said. "Let me know, Jack, if I can help with the stadium. See you both later."

Jack's blue eyes connected with Anne's.

"What happened in that meeting?" Anne blurted.

Chapter 5

The three conspirators entered the Greenville hotel through the revolving glass door and proceeded to the lounge in the back. They found a booth and Marge squeezed in between Arthur and Ridley, both attired in dark suits. Ridley ordered a Scotch and water from the skimpily clad waitress. The Beckley's asked for gimlets. The drinks were delivered on a small cocktail tray. Arthur paid.

"How'd we do?" Marge mumbled, puffing smoke.

"I'm afraid we didn't convince Jack Mayfield," Arthur said. "He's the one I'm worried about. His father organized the group of lumbermen that built the stadium. Their descendants may not be happy when they hear the stadium will be torn down."

"They're businessmen, Arthur. I think they'll side with us," Ridley said. "We'll have to wait for Tom before we know what happened in the closed session."

An hour later, when the table held empty glasses and an ashtray full of cigarette butts, Mayor Tom Brand came through the barroom door.

"Here's Tom," Arthur said. "He'll be able to tell us what happened. Move over, let's give him room."

Tom plopped his big frame at the end of the booth. Marge felt her slim body rise. Gad, he's fat, she thought. He wore a green sports coat and white shirt. Curly black hair billowed out of the open collar. Tom lit up a cigarette.

"What happened?" Marge asked impatiently. She didn't like

Tom, or politicians in general.

"Hold on for a sec, Marge," Tom said. "I think you'll like what I have to say. I'm starved." Tom waived for the waitress. "I'd like a cheeseburger and fries. And a glass of Oly," he said. After scribbling on her order pad the waitress sashayed to the kitchen.

"It's the biggest political issue we've had in years. Did you see all the people?" Tom said. The waitress brought the beer. Tom put out his cigarette and drained the glass.

What a slob, Marge thought.

"Jack Mayfield has drawn the line in the dirt," Tom said. "If he can't produce a team by the end of the month, the stadium and its acreage will be sold. There'll be nothing stopping us then."

"That's just what I've been saying to Arthur and Marge," Ridley said. "We have this in the bag."

"Not quite in the bag," Marge said. "Did you see that sweet little girl? I'll bet her father put her up to that. Damn it! How do we stop Mayfield and his baseball pals?"

Towering over the conspirators Arthur whispered, "I think we have. When the month's up we'll be able to buy the property."

Chapter 6

"Mr. Mayfield," Anne said.

"Jack, please."

"Are you allowed to talk about what happened in the meeting?

"Sure. Let's go over to the hotel lobby. I'll tell you about it there." Jack gently guided Anne's elbow as they jaywalked between cars to the hotel's revolving door. They squeezed in and were spun out inside. From there Jack led Anne to the cushioned chairs. The chairs faced Main Street. The lights of the cars and city hall blazed in front of them. They sank into their chairs. Anne's anxious face stared at him.

"OK, OK," Jack said. "Here's what happened."

"Wait a minute," Anne said as she put on her white rimmed glasses, and positioned her pen and tablet. "Okay, I'm ready."

Jack recounted how the councilors had rambled on about the benefits of selling the property. It seemed that he and Susan Byrd were the only councilors in favor of saving the stadium.

"Bottom line: Money talks," Jack said. "After the board's discussion I knew the council would vote to sell. All I could do was to make a desperate last minute motion. Fortunately they went for it. I have 30 days to get a berth in the Pacific North League and put together a team. Can it be done? I don't know, but I'm going to try. That stadium must be saved."

"We really must save it," Anne said.

"Why are you so interested?"

"My boyfriend is Dave Summers, a baseball player. He plays for a county league team in Junction City. He loves the game. He's very good. Because of him I've become enthused about the game. That's one of the reasons I applied for the sports writer position at the *Greenville News*. Now I get to write about him. Maybe he'd be a candidate for your new team?"

"If Burt, the new manager of the Giants, gives the OK then your friend will get an opportunity to try out."

"Burt would be foolish not to sign him. What are the chances of you getting a berth?"

"I think they're good," Jack said. "I know a couple of the owners, and they need a team. They'd like to have eight teams in their league, for scheduling purposes, you know. The Giants may be their only hope. Anyway I'll find out tomorrow. I leave tonight for Portland. So wish me luck."

"I do, lots of it."

"Say," Jack said. "If you were to write a story about Greenville getting a North West League berth, then it would be easier for Burt and me to round up players. Would you be willing to do that?"

"Yes! I'll suggest to my editor that the article run on the front page of the sports section. I think he'll approve," Anne said. "I want you to succeed."

Jack noticed the mayor and his friends leaving the lounge. They walked through the lobby towards the front door. "Uh-oh," he said. "That group is trouble." Jack motioned for Anne to look. Anne turned at the wrong time; she caught Marge Beckley's green eyes staring at them. Anne quickly looked away. "That group represents the money we're fighting. The Beckleys are the wealthiest people in town. Marge, along with many of her neighbors, will stop at nothing to demolish the stadium."

"A real trouble maker," Anne said.

18

"What's important now is for me to get that berth. I'm sorry, but I better get going. I want to be in Portland before midnight so I can find a hotel room and get some rest before meeting with the league's owners tomorrow."

"Please call me the minute you find out. Here's my card."

Chapter 7

Five days had passed since Marge and friends had met with the mayor in the Greenville hotel lounge.

Marge stepped outside to get the morning *Greenville News*. She picked it up off her porch and looked out at her front yard. Tulip petals hadn't been raked. The lawn needed mowing. The walkway was dirty. "Where's that gardener? For what we pay him he should be here every day," she muttered. She turned on the sprinkling system and then went back inside, her curlers bouncing under a pink scarf. Once on her couch, she glanced out at the east hills. The sun hid behind clouds. She adjusted her red robe around her skinny legs. With her gold lighter flaming, she lit a cigarette. She flipped through the morning paper, concentrating. She stopped abruptly at the front page of the sports section. Damn! She thought.

"Arthur, there's bad news!" Marge said as she put out her cigarette.

Arthur stooped as he came through the arched doorway into the smoky living room. He wore his brown bathrobe and black slippers. "What's so bad?"

"Take a look at the sports page. I told you Mayfield and that sports writer would spoil everything. Didn't you see them, Mayfield and that sports writer, in the hotel lobby the other night? They were plotting. Didn't you see them?"

"No," Arthur said, taking the paper from Marge. He read the first sentence aloud, "'Greenville Giants get a berth in the Pacific

North League.' This may ruin our plans." Just then the phone rang. Marge picked it up.

"It's Ridley," she said.

"Let me have it," Arthur grabbed the phone. "Yes, we just read it. I know, they've just passed the biggest hurdle in organizing a team. Now they'll have every baseball player that didn't make the major and minor league drafts trying out for their club. They'll be able to put together a team by June 2nd easily. Let me call Tom. He's sure to have some ideas about what we should do now. I'll call you back."

Arthur hung up. "Do you remember his number, Marge?"

She opened the drawer in the end table and pulled out their personal phone book. She read off the number. Arthur dialed.

"Hello," Arthur said. "Have you read the paper?"

Marge could hear Tom's booming voice. "Tell Marge not to worry. I have a plan. I'll call the city engineer when I get to the office. He can find something wrong with any building."

"Tell that engineer we'll pay him whatever money he wants," Marge said.

"Sssh, we can't do that," Arthur said, his hand covering the mouth-piece.

"They'd have to complete the repairs in less than a month," the mayor said. "Pretty hard to do, wouldn't you say?"

"Yes," Arthur said. "OK, do it as soon as possible. Call us when you have results." Arthur hung up. "I'll call Ridley and explain. In the meantime, we'll wait for the inspector's report."

Chapter 8

Jack Mayfield had no inkling of what the Beckley group was doing. Jack and Burt had to make preparations for the upcoming baseball season.

"What about Anne's boyfriend, Dave Summers?" Jack asked. "Anne tells me he's really good." Jack and Burt Andrews sat in the Giants' grandstand, looking out at the field.

"He's a natural," Burt said. "One of the best all-around athletes I've ever seen." Burt's experience playing catcher in the Pacific Coast League had immortalized him in the small community of Greenville. He had multiple awards for his performances. While in the league he'd batted an impressive .300. Jack never doubted Burt's assessment of potential players; he was always right. Burt was six feet tall, with an athlete's agile stature. He kept swiping back a lock of sandy-colored hair from his forehead.

"Some major league scouts have interviewed Dave," Burt said. "For some reason they leave without drafting him. I can't figure it out. If he tries out for the Giants I'll sign him immediately."

"Who else do you have lined up for the team?"

"No one has signed yet. Anne's article just came out today. I think we'll have lots of ball players since you got us that berth in the league. They'll come like bears to honey. My ad comes out in the *Sports Magazine* on Wednesday. A few guys have already expressed their intention to try out. On Saturday we'll see how many show up. From that squad, I'll pick two teams to play an intra-squad game on Sunday. I'll pick the best twenty-five or so from that session. We should easily have a team before our June second deadline. Plus we'll have enough time to get in some good practice before the opening game on June 15th."

"OK, I meet with our investors this evening," Jack said. "I'll fill them in on our progress. Meanwhile I've got to hire a grounds-keeper. We'll use the old Giants' uniforms, and we'll need a concessions manager."

"Make sure Ed Gilroy is our groundskeeper," Burt said. "His son played high school ball at Greenville High. I'd like him to play for us."

"I'll call Ed first thing. Anything else?"

"Let's touch base tomorrow. How's your business doing?"

"We're doing well, thanks to Bob Moore, my manager," Jack said. "He's keeping me free to work on the baseball team. I think the salesmen thrive when I'm gone." Jack laughed.

"How much can we pay the players?" Burt asked.

"Not much. We have two selling points to talented players: They'll be seen by professional scouts, and they'll be able to play ball this summer. We'll know Saturday if anyone takes the bait."

"Say, who's that kid with the shaggy hair?" Jack pointed his thumb toward a boy about ten or eleven years old coming out of the stadium tunnel.

"That's Mike Ward. His dad was killed in Vietnam. His mother lives on a military pension. They say she's been in and out of mental sanitariums. Schizophrenic, I guess. She keeps her drapes pulled all the time. Not a healthy environment for a boy to live in. There's rumors he sneaks out of his house at night. No one knows where he goes. Sometimes I think he lives here at the stadium. To look at him, you'd never guess he could play baseball. I've seen him though. He's tough as a rock and a good catcher. One of these days I'm going to teach him how to hit. Here he comes."

"Are you gonna have a team this year, Mr. Andrews?" Mike asked.

"Yes."

"Wish I could try out."

"We need a bat boy. Are you interested?"

"Yes, sir."

"Be here around noon on Saturday."

"I'll be here. Thank you."

"I'd like you to meet the man responsible for keeping our field available for baseball. Mike, this is Jack Mayfield."

Jack gripped the large hand, surprisingly large for his age. "Give me a firm grip, Mike."

"Yes sir," Mike responded.

"That's the way to impress your future coaches." Jack felt the young man's hand grip tighten. He looked into Mike's hazel eyes and thought he saw a sparkle of determination. Yet as the eyes darted away, and the hand dropped, Jack also detected a lack of self confidence.

"Why aren't you in school?" Jack said.

"That's where I'm goin' right now. See ya Saturday, Mr. Andrews." His scarecrow form, danced down the stairs and off he went, juggling three baseballs.

Chapter 9

That afternoon, Mike came home from school and entered the living room cautiously. His mother was asleep on the couch. On the coffee table were three ashtrays filled with cigarette butts. The smell of alcohol and stale cigarettes fouled the air as he walked into the kitchen. He flipped on the overhead light. From the refrigerator he pulled out a carton of milk. He pried open the slot and gurgled down three big swigs. He set the carton on the kitchen table. A frying pan was filled with leftover spaghetti. He turned on the electric burner and waited for the food to warm. Then he ate from the pan with a fork. His mother, dressed in a faded green bathrobe and slippers, suddenly appeared at the kitchen door.

"You're drinking out of the carton again. Won't you ever learn? We have glasses and plates. Why don't you use them?" Molly went to the cupboard and got a plate and a glass. She poured his milk and dished out some food. "There!" she said.

"Sorry," Mike said. He watched her as he ate. She poured some whisky into a glass. She mixed it with Coke from the refrigerator. Then she went back into the living room. Mike heard the table lamp switch on. He ate sparingly. When finished he decided to go to his bedroom. He put the milk carton back in the refrigerator. From the hall he noticed his mother lying on the couch, hands propped up on her chest, reading a paperback novel. When he got to the bedroom he heard her in the kitchen pouring another drink. He closed his door. The walls of his room were covered with posters of famous baseball players. Baseball paraphernalia lay scattered on the floor. Comic books were piled on his night stand. He took one from the bottom of the stack and sat on the edge of the bed. When his mother was on a binge like this he knew that he'd be in trouble soon. Sure enough, a few minutes later there was that familiar knock on his door. He put his comic book on top of the stack.

"Can I come in?" Molly asked.

"Yes," Mike said. She had a drink in one hand and a cigarette in the other.

"How was school today?"

It always started like this, Mike thought. "It was fine."

"You didn't tell any of the teachers I'd been in the loony bin did you?"

"No, mother," Mike said.

"Our neighbor next door said someone snitched on me, and it wasn't her. Did you tell your friends and they told the teachers?"

"No, mother,"

"Then why don't your friends ever come around?"

"I don't have many friends, Mother."

"But you've told them bad things about me, haven't you?"

"No, mother."

"You've told them I drink too much, haven't you? You've told them I'm a drunk!"

"Please. Mother I'd like to be alone."

"Ok!" She slammed the door shut. Mike heard her in the kitchen again. More whiskey he thought. He pushed his dresser drawer against the door.

KNOCK!-KNOCK!-KNOCK! "Let me in!"

"No!" Mike said. His mother pushed and shoved at the door. Mike pushed from his side and was able to hold her out. A few

28

minutes later she tried again.

"You ingrate, let me in there!" then she pounded her hand on the door. Mike held his ground. Finally his mother tired and returned to the couch.

Soon, she'd be asleep, Mike thought. When all was quiet, he put on his coat and climbed out of the window.

Chapter 10

Early the next morning, Jack's phone rang. He sat up and rubbed his eyes. After the fourth ring he lifted the receiver.

"Hello."

"Jack?" Anne said.

"Yes,"

"This is Anne. You're going to have to do something and quick. The city engineer has discovered major repairs that need to be fixed in the stadium. The city is threatening to close it down."

"Like what repairs?"

"It needs a new roof. There's serious water damage to structural supports, and the restrooms are contaminated. The inspector said the condition of the stadium represents a serious safety threat to the public. He estimates the repairs at $50,000 to $75,000."

"How strange that these repairs come up just before our season begins. Sounds like the work of the Beckleys."

"Are you sure it's the Beckleys behind this?"

"I'm willing to bet on it," Jack said. "Thanks for the alert, and I'll get on it as soon as I get to my office."

"What about Dave?" Anne asked.

"I've talked with Burt," Jack said. "Burt would love to have Dave on the team. Let's go for coffee on Friday and I'll update you on how everything is going. In the meantime, I'll be getting estimates for those repairs. It's a good thing I'm in the real estate business. I have a list of contractors that would love to do this work. The problem is coming up with that much money so fast. See you Friday."

After talking with Anne, Jack got dressed, topping off his attire with a snazzy white sports jacket and a blue tie that matched his eyes. At his office he called members of the Greenville Giants board. It wasn't long before he had gotten guarantees of $15,000. The board members also supplied him with a list of wealthy people. Within two hours Jack had raised the money needed. Next he called the contractors—a plumber to fix the restrooms, a roofer for a new roof, and general contractor to repair structural members under the stadium. Good thing the city council meets tonight, Jack thought.

Mayor Tom Brand called the business session to order. The six city council representatives sat at a large rectangle table in the council chambers. After a few contentious issues were tabled for later discussion, Tom Brand brought up the matter of the stadium.

"I have here a repair order from the city building inspector. He's listed items that need immediate repair before any baseball games can be played. If these repairs can't be completed in time for the home opener, then the baseball season will have to be cancelled. If the season is cancelled then the stadium must be sold. I must remind you the city has no funds to cover the cost of these repairs."

"Just a minute, Mayor," Jack said. "You're moving too fast. I've made preparations to have the repairs done before the home opener. A lot of preparation has already been made to get this team off the ground. We don't need more obstacles. Therefore I'd like to make a motion."

"Go ahead then," the Mayor said.

"I move that the city council lease the stadium to the Giants. I've contacted several teams in the league to come up with a reasonable rent. The Giants board of investors is willing to pay

$2,500.00 a month for the rest of the baseball season. This money will help our city and provide a stadium for our team."

"I second the motion," Susan Byrd said.

"Let's take a vote," the mayor said. "But, remember if you vote yes, the city will lose the option to sell the property. All those in favor of leasing the stadium to the Giants for a year, raise your hands." Four of the members raised their hands. "The proposal passes," the mayor said incredulously, shaking his head. "We're going to regret this."

Chapter 11

In the parking lot of the Giants' stadium, Jack was discussing stadium repairs with a contractor when he noticed Anne's red '72 Volkswagen bug drive into the lot and park next to his car. Anne got out of the car. She wore a white dress with a pattern of blue flowers. She looked stunning. Jack's heart skipped a beat. The contractor moved off towards the stadium. Jack and Anne met in the center of the parking lot.

"Hi," Jack said. "Did you come for that coffee I promised you?"

"Yes," Anne said. The wind tugged slightly at her dress.

"That's my blue station wagon next to your car. I'll drive," Jack said. Anne followed him to his car. Jack held the passenger door open. On the seat was a Mayfield real estate sign. Jack quickly tossed it to the back. Anne climbed in holding her pad and pencil. As Jack closed the door a familiar perfume tantalized his senses. Jack walked around the car and got in next to her. He tried to keep his eyes on the road as he drove the three blocks to Jerry's Café. Once inside they chose a booth with red padded seats. They sat facing each other.

"Two coffees," Jack said to the waitress.

"Cream?" The waitress asked.

"Black for me," Jack said.

"I'll take cream," Anne said. The waitress went for the coffee pot.

Jack squirmed in his seat. He definitely didn't want to make the wrong impression. He liked this woman. Plus he was very much aware that she could do a lot with her writing to help promote the Giants and save the stadium. The waitress came back, turned up their cups and poured coffee. Then she moved off to another table. Jack noticed she'd forgotten the cream.

"Sandy!" Jack said. "Cream, please."

"I'm sorry, Jack," Sandy said. "Here's your cream Miss, Mrs., er…"

"Anne Richards, sports reporter for the *Greenville News*. Thank you."

"Aw, yes," said the waitress smiling. "You're welcome." Sandy moved off with her coffee pot.

"How are the repairs going?" Anne asked.

"They'll be completed well before the home opener," Jack said. "Last night the city council granted the Giants a one year lease on the stadium. Tom Brand complained but he was outvoted. Listen, I don't know how to thank you. Since you alerted me early enough I was able to raise the money necessary to do the repairs."

"You don't have to thank me. I'm very concerned about the stadium. You know that, plus you know how much I want Dave to play for the Giants. He'll be very happy."

Oh yes, Dave, Jack thought. For a moment he'd forgotten about him. He wished Dave were in New York playing for the Yankees. Then he could ask Anne out. Yet Dave's talent may be the boost the Giants need.

"Burt has assured me that Dave will be on the team if he wants to play for us."

"Dave's playing ball this afternoon," Anne said. "Junction City plays Drain in a county league game. I have to write an article about the game. Would you like to come along?"

"Sure," Jack said. "Heck, I'll drive." Behind the wheel Jack felt more at ease. He asked, "How did you ever get the job of being a sports writer?"

Immediately Anne bristled. "Jack, I'm forced to prove myself all the time. Frankly I don't like it. I got the job because I was simply the best qualified person. Thankfully my editor recognized this. He cautioned me that it would not be easy filling what's usually thought to be a man's job. He told me, 'You'll be the Jackie Robinson on our news staff.' At first the resentment was strong, but now I think people are finally accepting me."

"Sorry for bringing the matter up," Jack said. "No more questions."

When they arrived at the baseball field's parking lot, Jack couldn't find a place to park. The lot was full.

"There must be two thousand people here," Jack said.

"They've come to see Dave play."

"We're going to park on the street." They finally found a space two blocks from the field. A long line of cars lined the road's edge. They walked back, dodging the oncoming traffic.

"I didn't know Junction City had this many people," Jack said.

"When the Greenville locals find out about Dave and how well he plays, they'll fill up that stadium, too."

"That'll make the investors happy," Jack said.

They walked from the paved street to the gravel parking lot. Their feet crunched gravel as they plodded towards the metal bleachers. The game had already started. People jammed the bleachers and thronged along the foul lines. Kids clung to the outfield fence like wind-blown tumbleweeds. People roared as the Junction City team made their way to the dugout in preparation for the bottom of the second inning.

"I'm a reporter for the *Greenville News*. Please let me through," Anne said. Jack followed as she pushed her way through to a grassy spot near first base. Anne pulled out her pen and began to write. "It's zero to zero," she said, pointing to the scoreboard in right field. "That's Dave, number twelve." She waved furiously, hoping to catch his eye. When Dave saw Anne he doffed his hat and his stocky body bowed. A big smile erupted on his round pumpkin head. Black hair hung loosely almost to his eyes.

The first batter hit a single into right field. The next two batters struck out. The next walked. Junction City now had a man on first and one on second base. From the batter's circle, Dave approached home plate swinging his bat, warming his muscles. He looked over at the third base coach. The coach rubbed his forearm—a signal to hit away. Dave stood in the batter's box and tapped his bat on the far corner of the plate. Then he lifted his bat over his big right shoulder. He had an easy manner that belied the tense situation.

Dave watched the first pitch zoom over home plate. "Strike one!" said the umpire. Dave stepped back from the batter's box and rubbed his hands in the dirt. He waited a second then returned. The catcher crouched behind him. As soon as the next ball was delivered the pitcher seemed to realize he shouldn't have thrown another fast ball. Dave's bat met the ball with such force the crack echoed through downtown Junction City. The ball took off like a rocket, screaming horizontally over the earth, crossing the outfield fence as it gained altitude. The crowd went nuts, cheering.

"You're right about this man," Jack said as he watched Dave gracefully round the bases. "He's fantastic." Anne smiled as she furiously wrote about the home run on her pad.

Her notes later included how Dave pitched a two hitter, and hit two more home runs that led the Junction City team to victory.

Jack stood with Anne on the sidelines when the game ended. Dave pushed his way through the fans. They patted him on the back and asked for autographs. When Dave finally got to Anne, he gave her a big hug.

"Dave, this is Jack Mayfield." Hands came together in a loud clap.

"Glad to meet you," Jack said. "Tomorrow are the tryouts for the Giants, at the Greenville stadium. Will you be there?"

"I'm looking forward to it," Dave replied. Then turning to Anne he said, "I'll be a little late tonight. I'm going out for a beer with some of the guys."

"Okay," Anne said. They hugged again. "I've got to get back to the newsroom and file this story. See you tonight."

"Nice to meet you, Jack," Dave said.

Jack nodded and they shook hands again.

Chapter 12

The day of the baseball tryouts finally arrived. It was staged at historic Greenville stadium. Photographers were snapping pictures, and Anne was interviewing players. Dave was in a line that included about fifty other hopefuls. At the head of the line was a big rectangular table. On the table were uniforms, caps, and other paraphernalia. Mike ran in and out of the dressing room carting big canvas bags filled with bats and baseballs. Burt sat at the table. He had a pen and a roster of potential team members. Anne maneuvered her way up behind him.

"Big day?" Anne asked with a warm smile.

"Sure is!"

"Did you expect this big a crowd?"

"No way, I'm amazed. All these guys are either kids just out of high school, or they've been rejected from other professional teams. Seriously Anne, these guys are the league's *rejects*. My job is to make them into a team. There's not much time. First I'll interview them. Then they'll compete for their positions. After that I'll trim the roster to 25. Tomorrow, we'll have an intra-squad game. From that game I'll choose the best players. So, step back, we need to get started."

Anne backed off, scribbling on her pad. She stayed behind Burt as he started the interviews. She waved to Dave, smiling.

"Careful of your language!" Burt roared. "There's a woman here."

Anne blushed, but wasn't intimidated.

41

"What's your name, and what position are you trying out for?" Burt asked.

"Tony Gifford. I play third base," the lanky young man said. He wore a Junction City ball cap pulled down over his eyebrows.

"How can you see?"

"It's the way I play sir. My cap never moves. When I pull the ball out of the dust people are amazed. They say the same thing once, but never twice."

"Sure, sure, what's your experience?" Burt asked.

"I've been playing baseball my entire life. Recently, I've played for the Junction City team in the county league. Dave Summers encouraged me to come. He thinks I'm good enough to make this team."

"We'll see. Go line up at third base. Next!"

Anne smiled at Tony. She'd seen him play in Junction City and knew he'd be a good fit for the Giants.

"My name is Ron Stewart." The next man was unusually small and angular. He moved stiffly, abruptly facing Burt at the table.

"How tall are you?" Burt asked.

"Five feet five. Because of it, I'm often walked."

"Can you hit the ball, though?" Burt asked.

"Yes, and I'm good at stealing bases. All I ask is a chance to try out."

"You'll be given a chance here, son," Burt said. "Go line up at second."

"My name is Richard," said a young man with a noticeable black eye. Draped on his arm was a sultry blue-eyed blond girl about his age.

"Who punched you?" Burt asked.

"No one. I got smacked by a car door," Richard said. "That's the honest truth."

"That's right!" the girl said. "It was my fault."

"It's okay Betty-Jo, you can forget it."

"But I…"

"Miss," Burt said. "Spectators are supposed to sit in the stands."

"Go on, Betty-Jo. Do as my manager says."

"I'm not your manager yet," Burt said.

"You will be," Richard said. He was a tall, thin youth with extra long arms and a thick mop of brown hair curling over his forehead.

"What's your position?"

"I'm a pitcher, probably the best pitcher that ever walked onto this field."

"Oh yeah, who says?"

"I do. In my senior year at high school I pitched the deciding game that gave our team the state championship. I shut 'em out with my buzz-ball."

"Your what?"

"My buzz-ball. It comes into the plate like a corkscrew, and buzzes. Catchers have a hard time catching it."

"We'll see about that. You know I'm a playing manager, and will be the team's catcher. I'll see if what you say is true. By the way if you're so damn good, why didn't the majors sign you?"

"Because I've had injuries. They think I'm accident prone. But if you'll give me a chance, I'll show you I'm as good as I say I am."

"You've got it. Go start warming up in the bull pen. Oh, be careful and don't trip over third base."

"Very funny."

"Next," Burt said.

Anne jotted down Richard's name. She liked the young man's swagger. She also wanted to check the high school record books to see if what he said was true. That would be of fan interest.

"Aw, Dave Summers, I'm glad you turned out," Burt said. "Finally a player who is as good as he says he is. Glad you could come. You'll play both first base and pitch when I need you. Okay?"

"Yes."

"One way or another I plan to have you on the field at all times. I've seen you hit, too. Just consider yourself a member of this team."

"I'll go line up at first," Dave said, aiming his pumpkin smile at Anne.

Anne watched Dave move out to first base. Next to her, Mike was busy giving out baseballs and gear to the players as they passed. She thought things were going smoothly. She noted that there was a sense of urgency. These young men knew they wouldn't make much money, but they also knew it would probably be their last chance to play in the pros.

"Mike," Burt bellowed. "I need coffee."

"Yes sir, I'll get it."

A short man with a huge white cowboy hat stood in front of Burt.

"This ain't a rodeo, son," Burt said.

"Yes, but…"

"What position do you play?"

"Second base. I've been playing on the Junction City team."

"You're a friend of Dave's then,"

"Yes, sir!"

Anne saw Burt glance out to first base. Dave was warming up. He stopped for a moment when he noticed who was at the table. Dave's thumbs instantly pointed down.

"Sorry son, but I've got three men signed up for that position already. Next!"

Anne watched as the men were interviewed. Burt pointed to the diamond if he decided to pick the man. For the rest he pointed to the exit gate. The last one, Duane Wilson, got Burt's approval and sprinted out to left field. He sported a big jackrabbit foot that hung from his belt. Burt turned to Anne.

"Duane played one year for the Boston Red Sox before he was sent down to the minors. He made the big leagues, every player's dream. That's why all these men are here. They fantasize about being drafted. For Duane, it was years ago. He must be in his late thirties now. Some players can never get baseball out of their mind. They'll keep trying out until they drop."

"Sounds like a good reason to wear a rabbit's foot," Anne said.

"He lives in eastern Oregon where jackrabbits are the size of deer."

"He's hoping to make your team."

"It's possible, but it won't happen because of a lucky charm. Some baseball players are pretty superstitious."

Anne thought Duane Wilson would be a good sports story. She saw Burt gazing out at the ball players. She wondered how much longer he'd be able to play catcher. He was getting older, too. After Burt shuffled through his paperwork, he stood and beckoned the players to his table.

"You all know that every position is up for grabs. There's more to this game than just hitting and fielding. You've got to master the sign language and be able to follow my directions. You have to prove to me you're the best one out there. And remember, this is a team sport."

Chapter 13

It was the next day. The intra-squad game that Burt had organized had just finished. The players had gone home. Burt and Jack sat on benches in the stadium's empty dressing room. "What a turnout," Burt said. "I never expected fifty players to show up. These kids have something to prove. They're underdogs in this league and they know it. They're hungry to win. If I can harness that energy, we'll have a shot at the pennant."

"I hope you succeed."

"I've seen it happen before. It can be done. Hey, that kid Mike Ward ran his butt off helping me. He shagged balls, readied bats, brought towels. I tell ya, he worked. I'm impressed with his enthusiasm. I've got to think of a way to repay him."

Burt's elbows settled on his knees, his face resting on two upturned hands. "That cocky kid Richard Macomb is a high school dropout. He's one of the best pitching prospects I've ever seen. Believe me I've caught some good pitchers." He lifted his head and tried to describe Macomb's pitch. "His ball, he calls it his buzz-ball, is unbelievable. It revolves and gyrates. I don't know where the damn ball's going to land—chest high or at the knees. This kid, I tell ya, should be pitching for the Yankees. "

"Dave Summers should be playing for the Yankees, also. I've decided to build the team around them. You should have seen Dave play. That kid hits the cover off the ball every damn time he's at bat. He's a natural talent in every position. The best all-around athlete I've ever seen. When he's not pitching he'll be playing first base. As long as those two are on the field, we'll win ball games. When Greenville baseball fans find out about them, they'll come in droves to see them play."

"We know Macomb is just out of high school, but what about Dave? Why haven't the majors signed him?" Jack asked.

"I don't know," Burt said.

"Maybe Anne can find out. She's been dating him. If he's got a criminal past we could be in for trouble."

"Find out, Jack," Burt said. "Find out fast, because our season begins next Friday."

"Good morning, this is the *Greenville News*, may I help you?"

"I'd like to speak to Anne Richards in the sports department?"

"I'll put you through."

"Hello, this is Anne."

"Anne I need to see you as soon as possible. Where can we meet?"

"The hotel lobby in ten minutes? What's up anyway?"

"I'll tell you when we meet. Bye for now."

It was a warm Monday morning. Outside the huge leaded glass windows, the traffic raced by. Jack sat in a plush red chair, wearing his usual white sports jacket, dark brown slacks and blue tie. Anne sat on the edge of her seat holding her pad and pencil. She wore white rimmed glasses.

"Why this emergency meeting?" Anne said, her blue eyes fastened on Jack's.

"I think we may have a problem." Jack uncrossed his legs and leaned forward. "Burt has everything figured out on how to field a team," Jack's eyebrows rose. "He's going to build the team around Dave. Dave is such an outstanding athlete that with him on the field we'll win games, maybe the pennant. If we could win the pennant then pro-baseball might be saved for this community. Plus the stadium will no longer be in jeopardy. My concern is this—why haven't the major leagues signed Dave? We know they've talked to him. If he has a criminal past we can't have him representing Greenville. It could destroy everything we've worked for." Jack straightened.

"A criminal past? You've got to be kidding." Anne said removing her glasses and putting them into her blue hand bag.

"Well, then why isn't he playing in the majors where he belongs?"

Anne frowned. "I don't know. I suppose I should try to find out."

Chapter 14

On Tuesday Jack received a call at his office from Anne.

"Hello Jack?"

"Good morning Anne." Jack said anxiously. "Any news about Dave?" Jack's elbow landed on his desk shoving real estate folders aside.

"Dave can't figure it out," Anne said. "He says he goes out for a beer with the scouts and by the time they're finished with the interview, they never ask him to sign up. He's really been disappointed. It's happened twice now. He swears he has no criminal background. He's a model citizen, even volunteers for the Junction City fire department. I just can't figure it out why the pros don't sign him. Honestly, I'd tell you if something seemed fishy."

"Thanks, Anne," Jack said as he sat up in his swivel chair. "I'm relieved to hear this. Our first game is Friday against the Portland Ravens. We just want to be sure he won't be a liability. I hope you understand."

"Oh sure," Ann said. "I think everything is fine. Will you be at the game?"

"I'll be traveling with the team. Hope to see you up there."

"I'll be there. Bye."

Chapter 15

Unable to sleep, Dave listened to his radio. It was 2 a.m. His sparsely furnished rental lay on the outskirts of Junction City. It was usually a quiet location, one of the reasons he'd chosen this house, but this morning the quiet was shattered by the siren of a fire truck. Dave's phone rang. He turned off the radio, and then lifted the receiver.

"Dave, there's a big fire at the grocery store, First and Main. We'll need your help. Hurry," the voice said.

Dave stood and turned off the radio. His fire gear lay on a chair by the phone. He threw on his helmet, and pulled on his fire overcoat. Once through the door he sprinted for his yellow Cadillac. The site of the fire wasn't far from his home, and as he approached he could see the huge cloud of smoke billowing skyward. The fire truck was already there. The other volunteers were hooking up hoses to the hydrants. The entire store was engulfed in flames. Chief Caulkins was directing the volunteer firemen. A middle-aged woman was screaming at him.

"Hurry!" She shouted. "My husband's in there! He was working late, cutting up meat for tomorrow's trade. He must have dozed off. The best way to get to him is from the loading dock at the back of the store. Hurry, for God's sake."

Dave ran up to the chief.

"Dave," the chief said, "take this axe and get around to the back of the store, to see if you can get in. Be careful. Don't risk your life. The rest of us have got to keep this fire from jumping to neighboring homes."

Dave galloped to the back of the store. Mrs. Bartel, the distraught wife, followed at a distance. The loading dock was cluttered with cardboard boxes and fruit crates. Flames shot from the second floor windows of the supply room. Ashes fell on Dave's helmet as he pulled off a thick glove and felt the loading dock door with his bare hand. "Ow," he winced. He replaced his glove and tried the door knob, but it was locked. Then he used his axe hacking furiously at the handle. When it fell off, the door blew off its hinges in a fiery explosion. Flames leapt out the door. To the gasps of bystanders Dave pulled down his face shield and raced headlong into the inferno.

He knew he didn't have much time. Debris was falling from the ceiling. He guessed the butcher's room was to the right. He hacked his way through another door. Meat carcasses hung from the ceiling. He could smell the burning flesh, and the swirling smoke was suffocating. He saw Mr. Bartel trying to get up. He was coughing furiously. Then he fell in a heap, not moving. Dave lunged for him. He wrapped Mr. Bartel's arms around his neck and positioned the body on his back. Then Dave hurried for the exit. As he fled the room, the ceiling crashed to the floor behind him. Dave was barely able to get out the building exit when he heard an explosion. He felt the impact of the blast and was forcibly blown from the loading dock to the parking lot below. With the weight on his back he crashed headlong on the paved driveway.

Bystanders and Mrs. Bartel rushed to his aide. They removed Bartel from Dave's back. Dave's nose was bleeding and his face scraped. People helped Dave get up. The crowd rushed from the fire. Mr. Bartel was laid out on the parking lot and Mrs. Bartel held his head in her arms. He was regaining consciousness, coughing. Mrs. Bartel cried and gently caressed him. Between sobs, she kept thanking Dave.

Glen Rawlins, reporter for the *Greenville News,* suddenly appeared next to Dave.

"Man, you're the hero! That's the gustiest thing I've ever seen."

Rawlins and people in the crowd were patting Dave on the back. Dave felt a little panicky at all the attention. He staggered past Rawlins to his car, opened the door, and fell in. He needed a few minutes to catch his breath.

"People are going to want to know," Rawlins said behind him. "Was this man a relative of yours?"

"Later, talk to me later," Dave said. "Right now I've got to rest."

"Yes, sir," Rawlins said. "I'll call you at home. Will that be all right?"

"Sure," Dave sighed.

Gradually the fire crew gained the upper hand over the fire. Water from fire truck hoses sprayed the wreckage. When the blaze no longer seemed a threat to neighboring buildings, Chief Caulkins came over to Dave's car.

"Glen told me you were here," Caulkins said. "Are you feeling OK?"

"Fine, Chief, just resting," Dave responded.

"Look," the Chief said. "You've got a big game coming up. Go home and get some rest. We can handle this fire now. Thank you for what you've done. We're all proud of you."

"Yes, chief."

"I'll call you later and fill you in especially if we find any clues about how this fire started. For now, we can handle it."

"All right, call me later." Dave said. Dave started his engine and turned on his headlights. On the drive home he mumbled to himself, "I've got to get refocused for the game."

Chapter 16

After reading the newspaper article about Dave's heroic rescue, Jack couldn't be happier. Dave's playing for the Giants would draw fans. Burt's idea of building the team around Dave was almost prophetic. The Giants' investors had to be happy. Jack could hardly wait for the home opener the next day at Greenville's stadium. No greater rivalry existed than the Ravens against the Giants. With a local hero playing, he knew the Greenville baseball stadium would be sold out. But, first they had to play the opening game of the five-game series at Portland.

A tenor in full military dress sang the National Anthem in front of an estimated crowd of 9,000—most of them Portland Raven fans. The singer's rich voice echoed off the walls of the huge baseball stadium. The Greenville team and Jack stood at attention, lined up along the line between third base and home plate. They stood with their hats removed and hands draped over their hearts, solemnly facing the United States flag in center field. Jack wore the traditional Greenville green-and-white pinstriped uniform. When the tenor finished and the cheers subsided, Jack and the players returned to the dugout. Jack sat down and crossed his legs. He fidgeted with his boyhood mitt. This was the first game of the season. He had good reason to fidget. The game promised to be a harbinger of the season ahead. He saw Anne and Betty Jo sitting in the stands behind the dugout, and waved to them.

"Play ball!" the umpire ordered. Then he crouched behind

Portland's catcher, Dan Stultz.

Ben Martin, Greenville's short stop, strode confidently to the plate. He glanced at the third base coach for a signal. The coach rubbed his hands, touched his visor and took off his cap. Then, Ben stepped into the batters box. Walt Thurmond's first pitch sped past him at ninety miles an hour.

"Strike one!" the umpire said.

The season had begun! We've done it! Jack thought with a sigh of relief. Burt and I have resurrected the Giants. He looked out at home-plate, the batter was waving his bat over his shoulder. The next pitch came in slow and outside. Jack winced when Ben swung the bat well before the ball reached home plate.

"Strike two!"

Ben smacked his bat on home plate. Jack heard Ben say, "You SOB, throw me another change-up like that and I'll hit the ball clean out of the park." The next pitch, a curve ball, whizzed towards Ben's head, he quickly dodged back. The ball just missed him.

"Ball one."

The next pitch was a fastball, sliding over the outside corner of the plate. Ben sliced air.

"Strike three, you're out!" the umpire said.

The crowd cheered. Left fielder Duane Wilson struck out also. Pitcher Richard Macomb entered the batters box, confident as ever.

"Come on, Richard," Betty Jo rooted.

Richard hit the first pitch. The ball skipped over the infield toward second baseman Joe Knowles. His throw beat Macomb to first base. The three outs ended the top of the first inning. The crowd stood and cheered.

The Giants' dugout emptied as the team rushed for the field.

"Pitching for the Giants this evening is Richard Macomb," said the P.A. announcer.

Richard's first warm-up pitch sailed high over Burt's out-stretched glove and slammed the netting behind home plate. Burt trotted out to the pitcher's mound.

"Relax, son. We don't want to kill anyone."

"I always throw one like that. Don't worry, I'll pull it together."

"Watch for my signals and pitch only what I say. Got it?"

"I got it."

Macomb's next pitch hit the dirt four feet in front of Burt, veering off to Burt's right. Burt walked to the mound again, and Jack could hear the cuss words spewing from Burt's lips. What-ever Burt had said seemed to calm Macomb because his following pitches started hitting the strike zone. While Macomb was warm-ing up, Greenville's infield players practiced fielding grounders.

Jack turned to Alex Burns, a pinch hitter sitting next to him: "What do you know about Richard?"

"I played with him in the state high school championships last year. He'd suffered injuries in the early part of the season. When he recovered he showed remarkably good ball control. His arm is really flexible, like a rubber band. He's able to hide the ball from the batter's view. I know because he's struck me out many times. Batters can't see his fastball until it crosses home plate, and then it's too late. When he throws his buzz-ball, batters freeze. If he stays healthy, he'll win games for us."

Jack watched as the first Raven batter, Bud Cordon stepped into the batter's box.

The umpire's hand rose abruptly at Macomb's first pitch. "Strike one!"

"What do you mean, healthy?" Jack said, watching another strike zip past the batter.

"Some of it he brings on himself by being reckless," Alex replied. "Like when he was driving his car a hundred miles an hour. An unexpected curve caused him to veer off the road and his car flew into a tree. The car wrapped around it. It hung four feet off the ground. He broke a leg and his left arm. He's lucky to be alive. His injuries benched him for that season."

"Strike three!" cried the umpire. Cordon threw his bat down in disgust.

"That was no strike!" Bud complained. "It was too low!" Bob Zorr, the Raven's manager, raced over to the umpire. They were nose to nose, chests touching.

"I could see that pitch from the dugout. That was no strike," Zorr said.

"Get back to your bench! Both of you!" the umpire said.

"Bull shit!" said Zorr grabbing Bud's arm and pulling him to the Raven's dugout.

Jack saw the outburst, but he couldn't help side with Zorr. The ball was low. That's baseball, he thought. The umpire is always right.

Richard struck out the next two batters. Unbelievable! Jack thought. I never anticipated we'd get three strikeouts in the first inning. The Greenville team trotted to their dugout. The Ravens took over the diamond.

"Dave's coming to bat," Jack said. Dave hit the first pitch with a line drive that smacked off the left-field fence. Dave scrambled to second base. The next batter was Ron Stewart, Greenville's second baseman. After checking with the third base coach, he faked a bunt. The Raven's catcher dropped the ball and Dave stole third. Ron bunted the next pitch. The ball dribbled along the first base line. The Raven's pitcher, Thurmond fielded the ball, tossing it to Don Wellington on first base.

"You're out!" The umpire said. During the commotion at first base, Dave ran home for the first score of the game.

Jack stood and cheered.

The game proved to be a tight contest right through the ninth inning. The Ravens had zero, and the Giants had one. In the top of the ninth, Dave hit a home run. The score stood at two to zip when the Ravens came to bat in the last inning.

Richard's first pitch was a fastball. It whistled towards home plate. Pete Gussy swung with such force it sounded like a rifle shot when ball and bat collided. The ball shot back at Richard's face so fast he didn't have time to raise his mitt. He shifted his torso back but not fast enough. The ball glanced off his forehead. It flattened Richard. He lay unconscious, and the ball rolled towards second base. Ron Stewart fielded the ball with a toss to first. But his throw was late. The Ravens had a man on first.

The team doctor and the ambulance medics raced onto the field.

"Bring the stretcher!" the doctor ordered. They carefully placed Richard on a stretcher and carried him off the field to a waiting ambulance.

Jack heard the siren's mournful wail as it sped to the hospital.

The new Giants pitcher, Tom Gilroy, couldn't stop the Ravens. They scored three runs in the last inning to win the game three to two.

After the loss, Jack rushed to the Giants dressing room.

"Hurry up and get dressed," Burt said to the players. "We've got to get to the hospital and see how Richard is doing. Damn! I wanted to win that game!" In frustration, Burt threw his shoe against a metal locker.

Jack and the team waited in the hallway outside Richard's room. Betty Jo and Anne Richards were there also. Burt was talking with the doctor. When he finished, he found Jack leaning against the wall.

"What's happening?" Jack said, straightening up.

"Richard is suffering from a concussion," Burt said. "He just woke up. The doctor says you and I can go in. Are you ready?"

"Let's go," Jack said.

They walked into the bright, sterile room. Richard was

propped up in his bed with a bump on his forehead the size of a golf ball.

"Did we win, coach?" Richard asked.

"No, but I bet we would have if you'd been able to duck that rocket. You almost shut them out. If you'd thrown the buzz-ball like I signaled, this wouldn't have happened. You would have shut them down, kid."

"Sorry, coach."

"Next time, follow my orders."

"I should have practiced those defensive moves you wanted me to learn. It's my fault."

"Don't worry about it. Just get better. The team needs you son."

"Is Betty Jo outside?"

"I'll send her in," Burt said. In the hallway Burt told Betty Jo that Richard wanted to see her. She went inside. When she came out the rest of the players went in. Then Burt huddled with Jack. "This is a terrible blow to our club. When a pitcher is hit like this sometimes the fear of throwing again is too much to overcome. He may be up and going in a week, or he may never pitch again. We'll see soon enough whether he has the guts to continue pitching."

Chapter 17

The morning after the first game of the season, the mayor's gang assembled in his office. The Beckleys sat on the green couch. Jason Ridley sat in a chair facing the mayor's desk. Marge was not happy. She smoked nervously. It seemed like all their efforts had resulted in dead ends.

"What can we do now?" Marge asked in exasperation. "The Giants have played their first game of the season. The stadium's been repaired. Our options to halt this season and bulldoze the stadium are gone. You told us this would be easy."

Arthur's eyes rolled upward. Ridley fidgeted. The mayor's chair creaked.

"You aren't the only person mad at me, Marge," the mayor said. He folded his hands atop his gut. "My backers are mad as hell, too. I have banks, chain stores, and builders all poised to act as soon as we can derail baseball at the stadium. Right now, I'm afraid we'll have to wait out the season. In September, we'll see where things stand. It's only four months."

"Their pitcher, Macomb, was injured," Ridley said. "Maybe there'll be more accidents."

"I can't stand another season," Marge said. "We've got to do something. Anything."

"I agree," Arthur said. "Let's see what happens in the next two weeks. If the team goes on a losing streak, they'll lose some of their fans. There might be scandals. All sorts of things could happen to undermine the team. We have to be ready when opportunity arises. What do you say? Shall we meet again in two weeks?"

"Yes, sure," Marge said. The others agreed by nodding their heads.

Chapter 18

The team had to rebound with a win, Jack thought. The Giants really needed Richard to recover. The first game in Portland had been close. It surprised both Burt and Jack that the team had done so well considering their roster of rejects. Now it seemed probable they'd be able to compete in the Pacific North League. The eight-team league was divided into two divisions: eastern and western. The Greenville team was a member of the Eastern Division. The Ravens dominated in their Western Division. The Ravens were no slouches; they had won the pennant the previous year. So when the Giants almost beat them, the Giants gained respectability. With the season still in front of them, who knew what would happen. The next game might be pivotal, Jack thought.

The home opener promised to be an exciting contest, staged in front of a capacity crowd of six thousand screaming Greenville fans. Jack proudly sat in the Giants' dugout. Wow, he thought, this is what baseball is all about—fans buying hotdogs and Cokes, the media airing the game on radio, and newspaper reporters photographing fans and players.

The public address announcer stated that Greenville's local brass band would play the national anthem. Fans stood in the stadium. The Giants stood along the first base line looking out to center field and the flag. When the band ended the fans loud cheer could be heard all over town. A full moon was cresting the eastern hills, with Jefferson Butte silhouetted to the south. Now it was time for the fans to sit down, and the game to begin. Jack noticed a smiling Anne, Betty Jo, and Richard in the grandstands, watching Dave as he warmed up on the mound.

While Dave pitched, Rudy filled in at first base. Dave pitched one of his best games ever. By the top of the eighth inning he had allowed only two hits. He'd smacked two homers that had driven in a total of five runs. Now at the top of the eighth, he had to hold on to the Giants' lead. The first batter, Pete Gussy, got to a full count of three balls and two strikes. That's when Dave hurled his fastball dead center over the plate. Pete didn't have time to react; he stood there in disbelief. Jack saw Burt grimace as he caught that pitch. The next batter, Joe Knowles, singled to right field where Sam Collins fielded it to second. Then, Hank Cunningham came to bat. Before the first pitch to Cunningham, Knowles took a big lead off from first base, hoping to steal second. Dave almost picked him off, but Knowles made it back just in time. Hank Cunningham smashed a hit that bounced right past Dave and through a hole between the shortstop and the second baseman. Dave was faced with a man on first and one on second. Then he walked Dan Stultz. The bases were loaded with just one out. That's when Frank Torge, pinch hitter, came to bat. The third base coach let fly a number of crazy hand signals, and Burt showed Dave a few as well. Dave threw a fastball.

"Strike one!"

Two more fast balls had Torge headed for the dugout.

Next up was Don Wellington. Burt signaled for a change-up, and Wellington almost fell down trying to hit the ball. Following the signals from Burt, Dave managed to strike Don out. In the bottom of the eighth and the top of the ninth both clubs went three up and three down. The Giants won the game five to nothing.

After the game, Dave Summers was flooded with kids vying for his autograph. Later, Jack saw him running for the dressing room.

The Giants won the next two games and on each succeeding night, fan attendance grew. Jack beamed.

In the last game of the series, Jack thought Burt was nuts in asking Richard to pitch again. But Burt told Jack that the quicker he could get Richard back in the game the better. Despite a black eye and a small receding bump on his forehead, he managed to overcome the first game's bad luck. His confidence hadn't been damaged by the blow, or so it seemed. He allowed only four hits. He struck out seven batters and permitted no runs. After the victory, Jack watched as a smiling Richard walked to the dugout. How had he recovered so fast? Then Jack noticed Duane Wilson's jackrabbit foot dangling from Richard's belt.

Jack stood next to Anne when she interviewed Burt and the manager of the Ravens, Bob Zorr.

"How do you explain this success?" Anne asked Burt.

"I really can't explain it. It's just wonderful. We've had some fantastic fielding, and our pitchers have been phenomenal. What can I say? In our first game Richard was hit in the head with a baseball. Tonight he wins the game. No flinching, no fear. This kid is gutsy. These players know this is their last chance to prove themselves, and they're putting everything they have into winning. Of course, Dave Summers is also an inspiration. I tell ya Anne, this team has great potential."

"What's your reaction, Bob?" Anne said.

"I simply don't believe it," said Portland's manager Bob Zorr. "The Giants bonding in such a short time shows great leadership from their coach. His selection of outstanding players from a list of rejects has me thinking twice about my own selection of players. My hat's off to them. Believe me, it's not easy to win four games against my club. But in baseball, anything can happen. Don't count the Ravens out yet."

Anne ended the interview by talking with Dave, and getting his take on the team. "I think once we shore up center field we'll be unbeatable," Dave said.

The Greenville News' headline read: "REJECTS TAKE FOUR STRAIGHT GAMES."

Chapter 19

After Dave's assessment of the need for a center fielder, Jack knew he had to do something. Gary Weld had a sore arm, and it affected his throwing and batting. He had to be replaced. Yet no one had surfaced to replace him. In the next five-game series with Lewiston, the Greenville Giants won three and found themselves in first place in the Eastern Division. During the series with Lewiston, Jack received a letter from a high school coach in San Diego.

Jack reported the news to Burt. A young man wanted to play for the Giants. He'd graduated from high school in mid-year. He needed a team to play on. His high school coach highly recommended him. Jack showed Burt the letter. The coach wrote:

Gentlemen,

Freddie Toll has played great baseball for us. His fielding is impeccable, and he hit well over .300 to lead our team to a state championship. He needs the experience playing on a professional team. I'm sure he's major league material. But most major and minor leagues have already chosen players for the year.

You won't be sorry if you sign him.

      Sincerely,

      A.J. Tindall, baseball coach

      San Diego, High School.

Burt instructed Jack to send a letter of invitation to the recruit. Jack received word back that Freddie was taking the train to

Greenville and asked Jack to meet him at the station. In the meantime, Burt had taken the team to Walla Walla, Washington, for a five-game series. That series would take the season into the first days of July. Freddie arrived Wednesday afternoon as scheduled. Jack met Freddie at the station. The young man brought with him his favorite mitt and great expectations of playing professional baseball. Trouble started when Jack tried to find Freddie a place to rent. Landlords began making excuses that didn't make sense. For example, "I have four applications on my desk, and haven't decided who to rent to yet." Or, "Sorry, I've already rented the place, don't bother me again." Or, "My brother has decided to rent the place, so it's not available anymore." Frustrated, Jack decided he'd try one more place.

"I didn't think I'd have trouble here," Freddie said. "I should have brought Rosa Parks with me."

"I don't know if she could've helped," Jack said. "I never realized Greenville had this level of intolerance. Let's try one more place."

"I'm not going back home," Freddie said. "I'll sleep in the park if I have too."

"It won't come to that," Jack said. "I guarantee it." They drove up to a single family house not too far from Greenville's campus. A "For Rent" sign hung in a second-story window. Jack and Freddie walked up to the front door and rang the bell. An elderly, heavyset woman answered. She rested her body on her cane.

"We'd like to take a look at your room," Jack said. "Is it still available for rent?"

"Yes," the woman said in a low, suspicious voice. "Is the room for you or your friend?"

"It's for my friend."

"Bertrand!" she yelled. Bertrand shuffled to the door from somewhere deep in the recesses of the home. A few strands of graying hair hovered over a balding head. His eyes were sunken, and looked as though they'd been blackened in a fight. His half-moon spectacles rested on the tip of his nose. He was taller than his wife, but walked with a hunched back.

"What is it?" Bertrand said.

"This black gentleman would like to see the room. Would you take him up?" Bertrand examined Freddie, slowly lifting and lowering his eyes.

"One of your kind, huh?" Bertrand said. "Follow me." Freddie ducked through the doorway. Jack noticed the contrast between a tall, agile athlete and a stiff old man. As soon as Freddie left, Jack knew he didn't want Freddie to live there.

A neighbor from across the street came up to the door. She'd been watering her lawn.

"Grace, I just wanted you to know I'll be trying to sell my house soon."

"He hasn't rented the room yet," Grace said gruffly. "I believe I'm required by law to show it. You understand."

"Thanks," Grace said and walked back to her front yard. She stared in their direction as she continued to water.

Bertrand and Freddie returned to the front room. Before anyone could speak, Jack said, "I'll be calling you if we're interested." He grabbed Freddie's arm and led him down the porch stairs and out to the car. Once in the car Jack said, "I've decided to rent you a room in my house. Would that be OK?"

Freddie grinned, then his face broke into a huge smile and his white teeth showed like a blazing neon sign.

"Yes, sir. You should have seen that room. It was filthy. The park would have seemed like the Hilton in comparison."

Jack grinned too, relieved. Then they both laughed. "Wow," Jack said. "I've lived here all my life, yet I didn't expect this. Phew! I'm glad it's over with." As they drove away from the house the neighbor stared after them. Once Jack was home he got the upstairs bedroom ready for Freddie. Then Jack called Burt in Walla Walla.

"Hi, Jack. I was just getting ready for bed. Bad news. We lost our first game with Walla Walla because Gary bobbled the ball, then dropped it, which allowed an inside-the-park home run. Two men were on base so they beat us three to two. Did Freddie arrive? We really need him."

"Yes. I rented him a room in my house. Otherwise we'd have a problem."

"What do you mean?"

"Burt, Freddie is a black man. Trying to find him a room stirred up a few Greenville citizens."

"What!" Burt fired back. "Bring him up here. We need him for tomorrow night's game."

"We'll be there."

Chapter 20

Jack sat in the Walla Walla dressing room. He'd driven up from Greenville earlier in the day, bringing Freddie with him. Freddie towered five inches above Jack, and had a lean physique. There was no doubt he was ready to play. He looked smartly dressed, too, in his pin-striped uniform. His right hand punched leather. The team members sat on the locker room benches.

"It's my pleasure to introduce our newest player, Freddie Toll," Burt said. "He'll replace Gary in center field. Gary's on his way home to give his sore arm some rest. Freddie will take Gary's place in the batting lineup. Tom Gilroy will pitch tonight. Any question about tonight's game? Yes, Dave?"

"Can I talk with you privately? It won't take long."

"In the hall then," Burt said. As Burt was leaving the room he motioned Jack to follow. In the hallway the three men came face to face.

"What is it, Dave?" Burt said.

"I don't play with niggers."

Jack couldn't believe his ears. He'd had enough of racists, first landlords and now this! He got inches from Dave's face. "You're off the team! Go pick up your gear."

"No!" Burt said, as he abruptly pulled Jack back. "I'm the coach here. I make the player decisions. Go back inside."

Jack returned to the dressing room and sat next to Freddie. Freddie hadn't moved. He just kept punching his mitt. He looked straight ahead, clenching his teeth. Freddie knew what was going on, Jack thought. "I'm sorry about this Freddie."

"It's not your doing," Freddie said. "You'd think I'd be used to it by now. I believe most of the players accept me. Unfortunately, this type of fanaticism still exists. Look at the recent slaying of Martin Luther King's mother, Alberta. Jack, it's unbelievable! Just because I'm black, people want to harass me. I won't be bullied. Someday it won't be like this."

Jack thought it must seem like a bolt of lightning on a clear night. BOOM! Someone hates you because of your skin color. Jack had a hard time comprehending this. Maybe he should have punched Dave in his big fat mouth. But for now, Jack sat respectfully, next to Greenville's newest player. Freddie was Jack's hero.

Players put on caps, oiled their mitts and checked their cleats. They were getting ready to leave the dressing room when Jack stopped them.

"Hold on a minute. Let's wait for Burt to come back. There may be some changes in the lineup." The players sat back down to wait for Burt.

Finally Burt and Dave came back into the room. "Now listen up, you guys, because I'm not going to give this lecture again. Dave threatened to leave our team because we have a black man on it. Dave and I have come to an understanding. We need him and he needs us. We simply can't afford to lose him. If you have strong opinions, keep them to yourself, because otherwise the pros aren't going to sign you. Dave is a good example of that. He's been interviewed twice and each time rejected. Maybe now he understands why. For Christ sakes, you assholes, the majors have been integrated for thirty years. That's a fact. Thirty years. Think about it.

"So, how do we deal with our current difficulties?" Burt asked. "This is how! We're putting the team first. If the team fails, then all of you fail. If the team succeeds, then some of you will have the opportunity to sign with the majors. If you can't control your feelings then *get off* the team now. I know that most of you have been dreaming of playing in the major leagues all your life. Isn't that so Dave?"

"Yes, sir," Dave whispered.

"Isn't that so, Freddie?"

"Yes, sir."

"And you Jack, your motivation is to save the Greenville Stadium, right?" Jack nodded his head. "Then the only way we're going accomplish our goals is to win a pennant. We have the makings of a championship team here, I sense it. But it's essential that we work together. Freddie comes to us with unbelievable stats. He's going to be an outstanding addition to our squad and will help us reach our goal.

"Before this season none of you had much hope of getting anywhere. Remember, the team comes first. Oh yes, one other very important thing." Burt walked over to where Freddie Toll sat. "We're glad to have you on our team." He vigorously shook Freddie's hand. "We need you, Freddie." The rest of the team came over to shake Freddie's hand too, all except Dave. Burt narrowed his eyes. "Now, get your butts out there and play some baseball."

Jack thought Burt had handled a difficult situation in a professional manner. There was no use in challenging Burt's authority. After all, he was the coach. Yet, damn it, if he'd been the coach he'd have fired Dave on the spot. Jack still glowed red, and couldn't help wondering how Anne could love this man. Maybe she didn't know about his racist views.

Burt's fiery lecture resulted in the Giants winning the next game with Walla Walla. The hero was Freddie Toll. He blasted two home runs and made some outstanding catches in center field. One happened in the top of the second inning. Tom Gilroy was pitching for the Giants. Two men were on base, first and second. There was just one out. Tom's pitch was a fastball and the batter had anticipated it. He smacked the pea towards the center field fence.

Like an antelope, Freddie loped after it. His concentration was on the ball. By the time he reached the fence he was going full throttle. Then he leapt in the air. When mitt and ball intersected so did Freddie and the fence. He slammed against it, yet still maintained control of the ball. When he landed on the ground he was on his back. He quickly arched up on his feet, like a gymnast, and seeing that the runner on second had left for home plate, he threw a line drive to Ron Stewart, the Giants second baseman. Stewart tagged his base. The Greenville news had it like this: "FREDDIE TOLL HERO! In his first professional game he single-handedly made a smart double play. Realizing the batter hadn't tagged up on second, Freddie threw a line drive to Stewart on second to complete the double play."

The Giants won the next three games, leaving Walla Walla stunned. Dave and Freddie teamed up for some of the best baseball heroics fans had ever seen in the Pacific North League. When the team returned to Greenville, Jack could sense the growing excitement. With three outstanding players on their team, making headlines every game, Jack knew his backers had to be pleased. Plus, the stadium's future seemed assured.

Chapter 21

When Anne heard from a Walla Walla reporter about Dave's outburst, she agonized over what to do. She thought she loved him. Yet could she tolerate behavior like this? There seemed to be some issues in Dave's personality that she didn't quite understand—a distance, a gulf that separated them. In baseball he excelled, a true athlete. But in their relationship Dave had a certain timidity she didn't understand. She noticed that he lacked confidence in some of the things he said to her. It was as if he didn't really appreciate her. Still, she felt close to him. She appreciated that he'd risked his life to save another human being. But did she want to reach out to him now?

Dave called her when he got back from the victorious Walla Walla series. He wanted to see her. Anne agreed to meet with him in the lounge of the Greenville Hotel at seven. She wanted to know how Dave would react when she confronted him. If he could not convince her that his actions had been misrepresented, then she was through with him.

They met in the lobby, as planned. Dave wore a blue suit and fancy red tie. He carried a big bouquet of red roses, in a green vase. Anne smiled at the sight of flowers, and couldn't help reaching out to hold and smell them. She followed Dave to a secluded booth in the lounge.

"It's really good to see you," Dave said. "I've missed you a lot."

"I've missed you too," Anne said hesitantly, her brow furrowing. She put the vase of flowers down on the table, then sat across from Dave. "I understand by the newspaper reports you played some fantastic baseball. The sportswriter in the Walla Walla paper praised you highly. He compared you with some of the greatest baseball players of all time."

"I hope some major league scouts read his summary," Dave said, resting back with his pumpkin smile spreading from ear to ear. "I'm waiting for that big paycheck."

"Dave, I'm really happy about your success," Anne said. "But I'll be honest with you. Something is really bothering me."

"Is it about the way I responded to Freddie being on our team?" Dave asked.

"I'm afraid so," Anne said.

"Listen Anne," Dave said, leaning toward her, his grin becoming serious. "I confronted the issue because I feared for the team's popularity. Attendance will drop off. I'm not the only one on the team that feels betrayed. Jack tried to kick me off the team. Had he got his way the team would be losing. I'll never forget that insult. Why bring in a black man anyway? We were an all-white team that had spirit, and we were winning."

"Freddie's introduction to the team has not changed anything," Anne said. "You're still winning. If anything, Freddie will help the Giants win a pennant."

"It'll ruin morale on the team. This is an American team," Dave said. "It's the whites that made baseball what it is today. The black men are foreigners. If we let one black man play for us then there will be more. Can't you see that?"

"No, I can't," Ann said. "I wish I'd known about your feelings before. I'd never have gone out with you."

"Anne, the opportunity to explain my feelings never came up," Dave said. "I'm sorry you feel that way. Freddie denigrates our team. "

"That's ridiculous," Anne said. Clearly agitated, Ann grabbed her purse and abruptly squeezed out of the booth. When she turned to face Dave her hand flung out in front of her, accidentally knocking over the vase. Water and flowers flew across the table. "Don't you ever call me again!" She turned, sobbing, and walked out.

Chapter 22

When Jack and Freddie got home after the Walla Walla series, they nodded and yawned as they made their way to their bedrooms. Once in his bed, Jack couldn't sleep. He worried about Anne. Should he tell her about Dave's racist views? Maybe he shouldn't interfere, yet he felt an obligation to tell her. After all, it was a horrible surprise to him. No one had suspected it. Maybe Dave had kept his views from Anne as well. Anne needed to know. It was ten thirty. Should he call?

"Hello," Anne said.

"Anne this is Jack. Sorry to call so late, but I couldn't sleep. I have some news I think you should know."

"Is anyone hurt?"

"No, nothing like that. I'd rather tell you in person. Could you meet me at Jerry's café tomorrow morning, say eight a.m.?"

"Sure. See you there," Anne said.

Jack and Anne arrived at the café on 17th and Main at the same time. The sun blazed in the east. When they met in the parking lot, Jack noticed Anne's eyes were red from crying. They walked into the restaurant. Their favorite padded booth by the window was empty. Anne was casually dressed in a white skirt and blue blouse. She wore a wide-brimmed yellow hat that framed her oval face. She was always attractive, Jack thought, no matter what she wore. They both sat in silence watching the traffic when the waitress came over.

"Coffee?" Sandy said, wearing a black apron, her hair in a ponytail.

"Yes," Jack said, "and cream." After bringing cream, Sandy filled their cups.

A dozen customers sat at the counter. The glass cabinets behind the counter were filled with freshly baked pies, and a tabletop burner held four coffee pots. The other two waitresses hurried about with steaming plates of fresh cooked food. The owner carried a coffee pot from table to table, making small talk as he filled empty cups.

Jack took a sip of coffee and knit his brow seriously.

"I wanted to tell you something you may not like. That's why I thought I should tell you in person."

"I know what you're going to say," Anne said, her eyes tearing up. "I know about Dave."

"How did you find out?"

"From a Walla Walla sportswriter," Anne used her yellow handkerchief to wipe away a tear. "He was in the locker room. He heard Burt's lecture. Last night I told Dave I never want to see him again. If I'd known about his racist views I'd never have dated him. It's as simple as that."

"I'm relieved to hear that," Jack said. "I somehow knew you might feel that way. Sometimes life just throws us a curve we're not anticipating." Then Jack smiled. "Now you've got me really curious. Why are you wearing that yellow hat?"

"I'm still recovering from last night," Anne said. "So I wanted to wear something cheery. You understand, don't you?"

"Sure," Jack said.

"My editor gave me the day off, too. He understands how I feel."

"Do you have any plans?" Jack said.

"No."

"I have an idea," Jack said. "My office manager, Robert, was asked to take a new residential listing, just last night. The owners to the property died in a car accident about a year ago. Their relatives live in Klamath Falls. They want my company to sell the property for them in order to settle their estate. Robert is going to Klamath Falls today to get the listing signed. He wants me to put up the 'For Sale' sign and do the measurements of the house. If you're not doing anything, would you like to tag along?"

"Yes, I'd like that. Where is the house located?"

"It's at the top of University Hill."

"It must have a view way up there."

"One of the best in town."

"I may want to buy it."

"If it's the house I'm thinking of, then I may want to buy it myself."

"You already have a house."

"Yes, at the bottom of University Hill. I'd like to have one at the top. The air's better up there." Jack said smiling. "I've got the keys, so let's go measure it up. You can hold the tape measure."

Jack's blue Ford station wagon pulled into the oversized driveway. The exterior of the ranch-style home was accented with white stone. Thick cedar shingles covered the roof.

"I want it," Anne said, smiling.

It was the first time she'd smiled since Jack had met her at the café. "Let's go take a look." They started in the living room with its thickly carpeted floor and massive stone fireplace. The fireplace's masonry continued up through an open, beamed ceiling. Jack had Anne hold the end to the tape while he jotted down room measurements. Anne exclaimed with surprise at each new room. The big master bedroom had a walk-in closet with storage shelves and dressers.

"Look, Jack. The master bath has tile floors and a walk-in shower. I love this place."

When they got to the kitchen, Anne's eyes opened in amazement. "I'm impressed, a gas grill, and built-in refrigerator." The room gleamed with colorful ceramic tile floors and every modern convenience.

"Jack, this is a marvelous place. I like the nook and the view out the window." She sat down, an elbow resting on the table as she looked out over the city of Greenville. Jack sat scribbling on his notepad.

When Jack looked up he could see the family room to the south. "Let's go measure the family room. Then we'll be done." It had another white stone fireplace and an endless view out its big windows.

"There's the university," Anne said, "and the stadium."

"That's Marge Beckley's roof, over there," Jack said, "the green house. Do you see it?"

"Yes," Anne said, her smile disappearing. "You know, Jack, I'm afraid something awful is going to happen."

"What do you mean?"

"Oh, with the Beckleys trying to get the stadium, our baseball team, and now Dave. I don't know. I can't put a finger on it. I just have this premonition."

"The team is doing better than it has in years," Jack said.

"I know," Anne said, taking the end of the tape measure and holding it against the wall.

"Don't worry. I think everything will work out."

"Oh, Jack, all this has got me thinking about Dave again."

"Sorry," Jack said.

"But, don't you see? What if I'd married Dave and we'd bought this beautiful home. What would have happened to me? It scares me to think about it. I'm going to be cautious about future relationships."

"I understand."

"How was he able to keep his hate from me? What a terrible trait. I completely missed it, Jack."

"I have some hidden personality quirks too, you know."

"What?" Anne said. "What are your quirks? I want to know. Come on, what are they?"

"I bat right-handed, but throw left-handed. I don't like broccoli, and my face goes into contortions when people mention tearing down Greenville's Stadium."

"Maybe you should wear a mask."

"I have a pretty funny mask right now, don't you think?"

"Jack, you're handsome."

"Do you want to know what I think?" Jack said.

"Yes."

"I think it is very important that you don't let Dave's problems influence your life. Forget him. You were lucky you found out about him in time. You have a life to lead, damn it. By being too cautious you might pass up a good relationship that offers genuine love, caring and honesty. Don't rule everything out. I care a lot for you."

"That's good," Anne said, "because I care for you too."

Anne's worried expression slowly left her face. She took off her yellow hat and sailed it across the room.

"You're right Jack, I should forget him." Then she stood close to Jack by the window. He could smell her perfume.

"If I had the money I'd buy this house," Anne said.

"If I had the money I'd buy it for you. Then we could go out on the town and celebrate." Jack put his arm around her shoulder. Anne's face tilted up towards his. Jack bent down and kissed her.

Chapter 23

Dave's expression hardened. He hated to lose Anne. But he couldn't hide his feelings about Negroes forever. Dave knew baseball was a mental game, and hoped he hadn't lost his confident edge. It was that edge that won games on the pitching mound. The one thing that bothered him more than anything else was Anne's closeness to Jack Mayfield. He had not only threatened to kick him off the team, but now had moved in on his girlfriend. Dave's hatred of Jack rose five degrees above boiling. "After this season," he muttered, "I'm leaving town." But for now he had to do his best, because the Giants were winning. The possibility of being picked by the majors still hung out there.

July passed in a blur of headlines: "Macomb's Pitching Quiets Bats," "Dave's Homer Wins Game," "Freddie's Fielding Saves Sweep." The fortunes of the rejects had made an about-face. Major league scouts came to see them play. No longer were they the scum of the league. Now they were heroes.

August began like July, with the Giants winning games. The Giants took three of five games from Bellingham and were in undisputed first place in their division. The Giants became the team others challenged themselves to beat. But, Dave wasn't happy. He wanted Freddie off the team. He felt they'd still win games. He decided to enlist his friend Tony Gifford, the Giants third baseman. Giff was the only other player on the team that had come from the Junction City club, and held opinions like Dave. Together they might be able to encourage other players to oust Freddie from the team.

At first, their efforts seemed promising. Dave thought the players were receptive. But when he'd ask them to join them, they'd clam up and back off. The other players refused to commit. Dave didn't understand what was happening until he invited Richard out for a beer. He knew Richard never turned anything down that was free, especially a beer. If they could get him away from Betty Jo long enough they'd make their proposal to him.

"Hey, Richard," Dave whispered after practice, "Lets go get a beer. I'll buy."

"OK," Richard responded.

Dave and Gifford took Richard to Lucy's bar in downtown Greenville. Dave ordered a pitcher.

"How's that rubbery arm?" Dave asked, pouring beer in Richard's glass.

"My arm feels great. It wins games for me. I don't think anyone can hit my buzz-ball right now."

"I know I can't hit it," Giff said.

"Me either," Dave said, filling Richard's glass again. "How do you throw that screwball anyway?"

"It's something to do with the motion of my body. I can't define it. What I'm doing is trying to make my movements fluid. Betty Jo says I'm the best pitcher she's ever seen. Her father is a damned good baseball coach, so I value her opinion. Betty Jo says if we keep winning we'll win the pennant." Richard drained another glass. "This town will go crazy. Greenville's never won a pennant before."

Dave refilled Richard's glass. It seemed an empty hole. Then Dave noticed Richard getting a little tipsy.

"I'd better use the restroom." Richard stood up, and wobbled towards the men's room.

"Order another pitcher, Giff, before he gets back. I'll ask the asshole after he drinks another glass. I think he's about ready.

What do you think?"

"I'm going broke," Giff said. "We better ask him soon." Gifford held up his hand to the waitress. From the new pitcher Gifford filled Richard's glass. Richard weaved his way back to the table and drained the glass. He's ready, Dave thought.

"Richard, why don't you join up with us?" Dave said. "We want Freddie off the team. He's not the right color."

"Right on, Dave," Giff said taking a sip of beer. Then he filled Richard's glass. "Richard, we need your help."

"What do you think about Fred?" Dave asked.

"He's playing great ball," Richard responded, the glass halfway to his mouth.

While Richard was downing the beer Dave saw a gleam of recognition pop into Richard's eyes.

"Oh, I get it now! You fuckers want me to help you chase Freddie off the team, don't you? That's why you asked me out for a beer. Wait 'til I tell Betty Jo this."

"That's right," Gifford said. "Will you help us?"

"I love you guys! I'd do anything for you. You know that."

"And we'd do anything for you, numb nuts," Dave said. "What do you say? Are you with us?"

Richard stood up, wavered around, and guzzled down the beer. Gifford was ready to catch him if he fell.

"Well, are you with us?" Gifford repeated.

Richard slammed down his beer mug. "No! I won't join the Ku-Klux-Klan!" Then he staggered out of the bar.

Even though Burt was using Dave more on first base than on the mound, Dave was pleased with the team's performance. Yet he still couldn't understand why his teammates wouldn't join him in ousting Freddie. Jack really had messed things up, Dave thought.

Now, because of Jack, we have a black player on the team, and I lost Anne. I can't understand why she thinks like she does. Women, I guess. I'd have done anything for her. The biggest insult to him would be if Anne started dating that SOB Jack Mayfield.

In the hot days of summer, the Giants were trampling over other teams like a herd of angry buffaloes. They buried Seattle, squashed Tri-City, stormed over Yakima, beat Lewiston, and clobbered New Westminister. The Giants were on a twelve-game winning streak.

Chapter 24

Many games had been played since Jack and Anne had kissed.
Jack didn't want too much time to slip by. Anne had said she
wanted some time before dating. He hoped now was the right
time. On the night before the important Walla Walla match up
he called her. He told her he had some important news to tell
her. Would she meet him at Jerry's at 8 a.m? When she accepted,
Jack knew he'd have to come up with some news. He decided to
reserve some seats for the series that next night, and invite her to
come. He knew she would be excited because Walla Walla had
given the Giants trouble all season. Still would that news really be
important enough? He didn't want to look a fool.

At Jerry's the next morning, with Anne sitting across from
him, Jack pondered that very question. Would she get upset with
him, thinking he'd brought her here under false pretenses? Jack
was trying to think of other news when Burt pushed through the
doorway. This was an unexpected godsend. They could talk about
the team's hopes for the pennant. Jack waved Burt over.

"Sit with us," Jack said. Anne's eyes seemed to question
the move.

Burt shoved into the booth along-side of Jack, while swiping
his blond hair back with his hand.

"I'm glad you could come," Jack gave Burt a noticeable wink.
"I told Anne I wanted to meet her here because of news concern-

ing the Giants." Burt recognized Jack's dilemma at once.

"Yes," Burt said slowly. "There is important pennant news."

"Well, what is it?" Anne asked, putting on her white rimmed glasses.

"That's it Anne," Jack butted in. "Even if we lose all the remaining games we're still guaranteed a playoff spot."

"That's right," Burt agreed. "That's our big news." Then he smiled at both of them. "I gotta go. I'm getting coffee for some team members. We're having a meeting in about five minutes. We need to get ready for the Walla Walla games. See you both later."

Phew! Jack thought and looked over at Anne. She was eying him suspiciously.

"I knew that!" Anne said. "Come on Jack, out with it. What's the real news?" Her wonderful blue eyes connected with his.

"More coffee?" Sandy said.

"Fill'er up," Jack said.

"No more for me," Anne said.

"I have two reserved seats for the three-game Walla Walla series. Would you like to join me?"

"It took you long enough. I'd love to."

Jack beamed.

Two victories and three nights later the Giants' dressing room was in chaos—players suiting up, reporters trying to get interviews, Burt rushing around displaying an upbeat, confident demeanor. After all, the Giants had beaten Walla Wall twice. He felt they could do it again.

"Hey, Duane," Richard shouted. "You got that rabbit's foot handy?"

"You're on your own tonight, kid. The rabbit foot stays with me."

"Dave," Giff said, "Think you'll ever get to pitch again?"

"Not as long as Jack Mayfield is sponsoring this team. He doesn't like me very much, and he knows the feeling is mutual."

"How's that ankle, Fred?" Burt asked.

"It's fine, coach. It wasn't sprained like we first thought. I'm ready."

A Portland sportswriter corralled Burt.

"Big news, huh!" the reporter said. "With your last two wins you guys are sporting a fourteen-game winning streak. It's unheard of. Are you going to tack up another?"

"If we win tonight, it'll be the biggest baseball news in this state."

"Who's going to pitch?"

"Richard Macomb."

"The whole league's waiting to see how you guys do this evening."

"I know, and with Richard pitching we should go right on winning."

"The kid's phenomenal. What's that pitch of his called?"

"The buzz-ball. I got to go. The guys are almost ready.

"Okay everyone, you have your assignments. We've got to back up Richard tonight. We can make history with this fifteenth consecutive win. What are we waiting for? Let's go get them!"

While Jack and Anne were getting adjusted in their seats, they watched the Giants run onto the field. The largest crowd of the season stood and cheered. Overhead was a blue sky and on the southern horizon loomed familiar Jefferson Butte. After the pregame ceremonies and the national anthem, everyone settled in for the last game of the Walla Walla series.

As the innings passed, Richard was pitching a great game. But, so was the Walla Walla pitcher. By the top of the sixth inning the game was scoreless. Richard struck out the first batter. Jack leaned forward, almost dropping his beer. The next batter waved his bat anxiously and stared at Richard. Richard's throw buzzed towards the plate. Contact was made and the ball zoomed across the ground towards second base. Ron Stewart swiftly fielded it as the base-runner neared first. It would be a close call. Yet the combination of second baseman to first baseman usually was a dead certain out, Jack thought. No problem here. He looked away briefly only to find Anne standing and yelling.

"That was an out! Jack, did you see that?"

"I looked away. What happened?"

"The umpire called him safe. Jack, I swear to you that man was out." Burt threw off his catcher's garb and hustled over to first base to contest the call. Most of the players chased after the umpire who had fled to right field. Then they huddled around him. Dave threw his mitt on the ground in a rage. Gifford and Stewart were yelling obscenities. The loud boos from the fans could be heard as far away as downtown Greenville. Still, two players stayed clear— Richard on the pitching mound and Fred in center field.

"Play ball!" the home plate umpire ordered.

The shout gradually calmed the ruckus. This was one time that Jack knew the umpire had made a mistake. The unanimous outcry from the spectators made it pretty obvious. He could see the smirks on players in the Walla Walla dugout. Dejectedly the players returned to their positions, and the fans to their seats.

"I think the umpire was picking his nose," said a fan behind Jack.

"He missed the call," said another.

"That's baseball. I guess umpires make mistakes too." Said another.

So, the game proceeded with one out and a man on first. The first base runner kept taking big leads off first. Richard and Dave almost got him once. The runner annoyed Richard's concentration. His third pitch nicked the batter's elbow. The umpire pointed to first base. Now Richard faced a man on first and second. The next batter hit a pop fly that was caught by Ben Martin at

94

short stop. Two outs, two men on. Burt erred on the next pitch and allowed the ball to get by him. The runners advanced to third and second. The next batter hit a blooper into right field that landed safe and it drove in one run. Then Richard struck the next man out.

The final innings found no runs by either team. So Walla Walla won the last game of the series one to nothing. The loss was taken hard by the Giants because it ended their winning streak.

"An umpire's error caused the Giants to lose," Jack said as he drove to Anne's apartment. He noticed Anne nod. Soon they were face to face at her front door.

"The next series is with Spokane, away games," Jack said. "After that we have the big series against the Portland Ravens."

"The winner of that series will probably win the pennant," Anne said. "Thanks, Jack, for an exciting evening."

"Let's do it again," Jack said.

"When the Ravens come to town?"

"Yes," Jack bent down and kissed Anne goodbye.

Chapter 25

After winning the series three games to two with Spokane, Dave had that night and the next day off before the series with Portland. He returned home to Junction City on a personal high. Besides batting over .300, he had a string of home runs. His numbers looked good. Surely he'd soon be noticed by the majors. After all, as coach Andrews had said, "If the Giants win a pennant all the scouts will be watching us."

Dave looked out the back window of his small house. The view extended across miles of farmland to the mountains of the Coast Range. The sun was setting in the west, slowly disappearing behind the jagged ridgeline. Dave felt that a celebration was in order.

Dave called two of his Junction City pals—Gifford and Robert. They agreed to meet at the Nahato Tavern in about an hour. Dave drove his 1970 yellow Cadillac west fifteen miles before arriving at the tavern. The highway that connected Greenville with the Pacific Coast ran through the small lumber town. Two buildings edged the highway, a grocery store and a tavern. The tavern saw heavy use.

The scruffy log tavern, with its peeling paint and ripped vinyl booths, provided the only eating and drinking place in the area. Loggers and mill workers flocked to the tavern after their shifts. Remote, antiquated, and rough, the tavern had its own ancient brand of human values. Dave could remember saying to his friends, "It's like walking fifty years back in time." Huge log trucks whooshed by outside.

Half a block from the tavern sat the lumber mill. Closed for the day, the usually busy mill looked like an abandoned movie set. Chain conveyers and forklifts sat idle. Smoke stacks jutted skyward. Log piles soared so high they resembled buildings themselves.

Dave loved this place. He enjoyed being with the unshaven, motley mix of loggers and mill workers. They wore their cork boots and plaid shirts. Many of the loggers had seen Dave play baseball. Dave was their hero. Dave felt at home in the tavern, not only because they appreciated his athleticism, but because they seemed to share his values.

He had a night and a day off before the series with Portland, so he planned to have as much fun as possible. He arrived before his buddies and parked in the crowded lot just east of the tavern. A sign on top of the gabled roof read, "NAHATO TAVERN— Music, Food, Pool." Also on the sign was a cartoon figure of a lumberman with a big axe resting on his shoulder. Beer and Pepsi neon signs flashed on and off from small windows. The door hung open. Just before stepping over the threshold Dave noticed the years-old sign over the door. "No Niggers." Yes, he thought, another reason I love this place.

Once inside the door, it took forever for his eyes to adjust to the low light. He heard the click of pool balls, and men talking. At last he could see the happy red faces. One light bulb hung over the bar. Another hung on a long black cord over the pool table. Men sat with their glass of beer in one hand and a cigarette in the other. Dave found an empty table and wrestled up some chairs. Smoke hung in the air like a Pacific fog. A jukebox droned in the corner. He sat down. The bartender brought him a glass of beer. A few men came over to shake his hand and pat him on the back. Dave felt good. He waited for his friends.

Soon, Robert Drew walked though the door, followed by Tony Gifford, his ball cap pulled to his eyebrows. They stood there for a few minutes getting their bearings. Robert played for the Junction

City team. He'd been unable to make the Giants' roster.

"Over here!" Dave hollered.

"Hey, Dave." Gifford was dressed in jeans and a brightly colored plaid shirt.

Robert followed, wearing a big white cowboy hat that made up somewhat for his short build. Robert held out his hand. They shook hands as friends do. Two more glasses of beer showed up on the table. The friends leaned forward so they could hear each other talk.

"How are the Giants doing?" Robert asked. "I've been so busy at the mill I haven't had time to read the sports pages."

"You lying midget," Gifford said. "You haven't heard? We had a 14-game winning streak going. We would've had 15, but for a shitty umpire call."

"Macomb was robbed!" Dave said.

"Hey, what about Macomb?" Giff said. "That asshole's putting up some good stats. I pity the batters that try to hit his buzz-ball. He's shutting teams down. I hope he's around for the pennant championship."

"He's scheduled to pitch against the Ravens in two nights," Dave said. "We can chalk that one up as a win." Dave turned to Robert, "I wish we could get you on the roster. We'd have fun, the three of us."

"Heck, I miss you guys too," Robert said. "The Junction City team is really down since you guys left. We've lost the last five games."

A pitcher of beer landed on their table. Dave filled the glasses.

"The team will pull out of it," Dave said as he gulped beer. Then he looked at Giff. "Duane Wilson is playing good. He got hits in the last ten games."

"Let's play some pool, you want to?" Robert asked.

"Those guys are getting ready to leave," Dave said, sipping his beer. The men at the pool table hung up their sticks and moved to the bar. The three friends took over, grabbing the cues. "Set 'em up, Robert. How about eight ball?"

"Sure, rack em up," Giff said. He took the cue ball, lined up his first shot, and smashed it into the center of the 15-ball triangle. Balls exploded over the table. A few went into the corner pockets. Giff took a gulp of beer and lined up for another shot.

"Jesus! Look what just walked in," Robert said.

Dave had been concentrating on the table. Now he looked up. He saw a black man walk past them towards the bartender. "Hold up," Dave said. Chatter stopped while everyone watched the black man. The only noise in the place came from the juke box playing a Johnny Cash song, "Folsom Prison."

"I need to use your phone," the black man said. "I'm out of gas. I have to call my wife in Greenville. You're the only place open."

"Sorry, the phone's out of order," Larry Bales, the proprietor, said.

"Will anyone let me siphon some gas so's I can get home?" the black man asked aloud.

Customers continued to gape. No one responded. The music droned on.

"Listen, ah, what's your name?" Larry said.

"George," the black man said.

"Did you read the sign over the door, boy?"

"No," George said.

"Well then maybe this one over the bar should explain everything," Larry pointed up. A sign over a spiked logger's chainsaw read, "Nigger handcuffs." "If I were you, George, I'd slowly back out of this place, before someone decides to enforce the pub's rules."

Dave could see George was frightened. He shifted from foot to foot. George seemed uncertain of what to do next. Why he'd come into this hornet's nest Dave couldn't figure. George kept looking at everyone with pleading eyes, hoping someone might help. No

100

one responded. As he slowly backed up toward the door, a man at the bar stuck out his foot. George tripped and fell. Some customers at the bar picked George up and held him. Larry moved over from behind the bar.

A chant erupted, "Fight, fight, fight!"

"Who wants to tangle with this nigger?" Larry said.

Dave stepped forward.

"I don't want to fight anybody! Let me go!" George said.

"Everyone outside!" Larry said. "We'll form a ring around them." George was dragged outside and placed in the center of the human circle. The ringside audience all held mugs of beer and followed Larry's lead. Dave took off his shirt and stood close to the edge of the ring. George slowly unbuttoned his shirt. His six-foot frame was chiseled and muscular, more lean and angular than stocky. Dave, on the other hand, had a bull's neck and a robust torso. His black hair fell loosely over his forehead. His usual pumpkin smile became a sneer. His deep brown eyes stared menacingly at George. Dave wanted this fight.

Fear seemed to ebb from George's face. Yet he was uneasy. The fight was inevitable. George had to face it. Larry brought the two fighters together in the middle of the circle.

"On this side we have George." Boos resounded upward, evaporating into the nights darkness. "George broke the rules of the Nahato Tavern. So he must be punished." More loud boos. The outside tavern lights glared down on the crowd changing them into long ugly shadows that danced eerily on the parking lot. "On this side we have the hero of Nahato Tavern. He's our number one man, a friend and compatriot, the great Dave Summers." Cheers echoed down the street. A log truck rumbled past, its horn blasting wildly.

Larry stood between the two men. "When I give the word, begin fighting." Then he looked at the crowd. "No one is to help or interfere with this fight. Is that understood?" Larry feverishly winked an eye. "Fight!"

The two fighters cautiously circled. Dave threw a couple of left jabs to the face. They bounced off George's jaw. Then a left hand landed in George's mid section. Air burst out of George's mouth. He bent over, but quickly recovered. A flurry of punches followed. Then a right to George's mouth knocked him off his feet. Larry held Dave back as George scrambled up. Dave continued to throw lefts to the face, and followed with wild right punches. George covered his face and deflected many blows. He was doing very little damage to Dave. The crowd loved it. Until George uncorked a right hand that sent Dave sprawling across the blacktop. Dave's nose bled profusely. Dave immediately was back on his feet. Now the two combatants held nothing back. It was a fierce struggle. They were standing toe to toe in the center of the circle, punching furiously. As each punch landed the crowd became frenzied, and screamed support for Dave. Finally Dave threw a right uppercut that landed squarely on the bottom of Georges chin. The punch held so much force that Dave watched as George's body arced up and away from him, landing with a thud on the parking lot. George lay there, unable to move. Shadows in the crowd kicked at his face and ribs. Larry pushed the rioters aside checking to see if George was alive.

"He's breathing. Let's move him to the side of the parking lot." Dave and a few men helped. The rest of the crowd returned to the tavern. About half an hour later Dave checked on George. He was gone.

Chapter 26

The newspaper office phone rang.

Who could be calling this time of night? Anne lifted the receiver to her ear.

"The town of Nahato is on fire," an excited voice shouted into the phone. "The lumber mill is ablaze and the tavern is almost gone. Fire trucks are on their way. You might want to send someone out there."

"Yes, we will! Thank you," Anne said.

Anne called the managing editor.

"Grab Stubs Brown and get out there fast. And be careful!" the editor ordered. Fortunately, Stubs was in the office developing film.

"Get your camera, Stubs," Anne said. "We're going out to a big fire in Nahato. We've got no time to lose." Stubs threw his camera bag over his shoulder, grabbed his tripod, and ran after Anne. They stuffed their gear in the front storage compartment of the little red Volkswagen. Driving west, Anne could see the fire's glow lighting up the western sky. "That fire could be the biggest in Emerald County history. I hope they contain it before it reaches the surrounding forest." As they sped through the sleeping town of Atenev, the glow grew brighter. The Volkswagen curved around the winding road and climbed over the forested hills. Her car lights bounced off of huge fir trees and alders that hung over the road. She pushed her VW as fast as it would go. As they neared the fire she slowed. The only place to park was in the parking lot at the Nahato tavern. She immediately got out, looking for people to interview. Stubs unpacked his gear. He set up his tripod and mounted the camera. He was taking pictures while Anne looked around. The tavern billowed smoke in front of her.

The front door frame was still intact with its notorious sign above it. "What!" Anne gasped. "Jesus!" She shook her head in disbelief. She had Stubs take a picture of it. Then she followed him to the burning mill.

The lumber and log piles burned with fury, sending blades of fire upwards. Smoke surged from the sawmill's innards. Ashes flew over Anne's head. Some dropped, sizzling, beside her. Anne was breathless. The fire reminded her of the infernos that had destroyed Oregon's coastal cities in the '20s and '30s. It was apparent to Anne that nothing would quell this fire. Red lights flashed from the tops of the fire trucks along the road. Firemen held hoses spraying water. The chief stood by one vehicle issuing orders. He wore a red fire hat and a yellow fireproof coat with a big badge. Anne waited for an opening.

"Chief, I'm writing an article on the fire. What's your name?"

"Wilbur Calkins."

"What's the damage?"

"Incalculable," Wilbur said. "It's definitely the work of an arsonist. My men have found gasoline-soaked rags. This fire was planned. I'd say the person responsible knew exactly what he was doing. He wanted complete destruction. He got it."

Anne wrote furiously. "Can you contain it?"

"I hope we can have it under control by morning. That's if sparks and flames don't find their way into the nearby forests. That's my biggest concern right now, to save lives and prevent a forest fire. We've had people evacuate their homes within a mile radius. As far as we can determine there's been no casualties."

"Chief," Anne heard a familiar voice from the darkness. Dave emerged into the light. "The nearby residents have been evacuated. Except for one old fool who won't leave." Dressed in firemen's clothes, Dave faced the fire chief.

"How about the mill's owner. Is he here yet?" The chief asked. "What's taking him so long, anyway?"

"He was at a meeting in Salem," Dave said. "We contacted him about an hour ago. He should be here soon."

That's when Anne noticed the bandage over Dave's nose. "What happened to your face?"

"I took a sucker punch to the nose," Dave said.

"Did that happen before the fire?" The chief asked.

"About an hour before the fire started," Dave said. "Right here in the tavern parking lot."

"Why were you fighting?" Anne said.

"Could the man you fought have set the fire in revenge?" the chief asked, butting in again.

"He had a gas can," Dave said. "And probably hated everyone in Nahato. What else would you expect from a nigger."

"What?" Anne gasped. She stared in disbelief at Dave.

"Chief!" Another firefighter pushed his way through the crowd. "We've found a body out behind the mill. We're pulling it away from the fire. He's pretty badly scarred."

"Can you tell if he's a white man?" The chief asked.

"Yes, he's white, chief."

"Why were you fighting?" Anne asked Dave.

"You wouldn't understand."

"I do understand," Anne said.

"Listen, I don't have time for a cross-examination," Dave said with a scowl. "I have work to do." Then Dave turned to the chief, "I'll go check on that old fool, gotta get him out of that house."

"Wait a minute, Dave," the chief said. "Do you know the black man's name?"

"Yes, he said his name is George, and he has family in Greenville."

"I'll radio this information to the Greenville police. Maybe it's not too late to round George up. I'd like to hear his story. We're now looking at a case of arson and murder. Dave, I appreciate your volunteer work. Go get some rest. Remember you have a big game tomorrow. And you've got to get a doctor to look at your nose."

"Thanks, chief. I'll check on that old man first." Dave disappeared into the darkness.

Anne didn't understand. Dave exhibited intolerance of the worst kind by beating up George, yet he volunteered to help out on fires. She thought it didn't make sense. How could a man be so thoughtless and thoughtful at the same time? Suddenly another man rushed up to the chief.

"I'm Larry Bales, proprietor of the Nahato tavern. Just wanted you to know, chief, there are twenty people who saw that nigger carrying a gas can towards the mill tonight."

"Thanks Larry, I'll definitely be in contact," the chief said.

Then a man pushed his way through the crowd, wearing thick black suspenders over a plaid shirt. "I'm the owner of the mill."

"Mr. Lofton, I'm sorry to report there's not much left. I hope you have insurance," the chief said.

"Yes I do, and they're going to be out millions," Mr. Hugh Lofton locked his thumbs around his suspenders.

"Do you know if any of your employees worked last night?" The chief said.

"Only Sam Taylor, the night watchman," Lofton said. "Why?"

"I'll have one of my men take you over to a body that's been found. We have to know who that man was." While Lofton was gone, the chief issued more orders. When Lofton returned, his face was crestfallen, and his wet cheeks glistened from the fire's glow.

"That's Sam all right," Mr. Lofton said. "I'm thinking this fire is a deliberate act."

"That's right Mr. Lofton, it's looking like a case of arson and murder."

"Any clues?" Mr. Lofton said, wiping his cheeks with his red handkerchief.

"Right now the best clue is that a black man named George was seen by twenty people carrying a gas can towards the mill. Plus we have a motive—revenge for being made a fool of at the Nahato tavern."

Chapter 27

"Good morning, Jack," Anne said over the phone.

"Good morning," Jack responded.

"Meet me at Jerry's in fifteen minutes. I have some very important news to tell you."

"Sure, see you there."

Jack and Anne sat staring out the window in Jerry's café. The back side of JERRY'S CAFÉ red neon sign flashed on and off over their heads. Cars flashed by. Anne briefly filled Jack in on the Nahato fire.

"Glen Rawlins, our Greenville News reporter, arrived in Nahato shortly after Stubs and I. His investigation has revealed that the tavern's owner, Larry Bales, incited the crowd, and that Dave beat up George. I don't care if George is the man who set that terrible fire, he didn't deserve a beating. No way do I condone that type of behavior. Rawlins has verifiable accounts of why the fight started, and Larry and Dave's involvement."

"I'm not surprised," Jack said. "I saw how he reacted to Freddie at Walla Walla. My God, Anne, I can't believe all this is happening."

"I know," Anne said. "My article will cover the fire, and Glen's will be about the fight at the tavern, and the sign found in the ashes. This morning Dave called me. He wanted to talk. I told him there's nothing to say. His actions last night confirmed everything. I hung up on him. I made such a big mistake by dating that man. He seemed so nice."

"More coffee?" Sandy said holding a fresh pot above them.

"Sure," Jack said. As she filled their cups, customers started filtering in.

"I think I've finally figured Dave out," Anne said. "I knew there was something about him I didn't understand. I sensed there was something he was holding back. It's all so clear now that I'm away from him."

"The man has many sides to his personality," Jack said. "Tomorrow night's game will be the biggest of the season. Scouts from the major leagues will be here. The stadium is sold out. I'm hoping Dave's not rushed off to jail for his fight with George. The team needs him."

"I doubt it," Anne said. "It's funny how the law bends over backwards treating athletes more favorably than the average citizen. You know, boys will be boys, or something like that. The fight and its underlying reasons are secondary to the big fire. Poor George was in the wrong place," Anne said.

"This whole thing is going to have a profound effect on Freddie," Jack said. "He won't take these affronts sitting down. I know Freddie. He's a fighter, and if he believes George has been framed then he'll stand solidly in his corner. Freddie's not afraid of anybody, including Dave."

"How will he protect George?"

"Maybe by contacting the NAACP. He'll find a way. He won't be intimidated."

"I wonder if Dave's playing will suffer tomorrow night?"

"He'll be trying his best," Jack said. "I think he truly wants to be signed with the big leagues. He's a natural athlete. I feel certain he'll make it someday. What time will you be ready?"

"6 p.m."

Chapter 28

It was the morning before the big game.

Recent events had created an opportunity for the mayor's group to meet. Marge and Arthur sat on their couch. Ridley and the mayor sat on living room chairs facing the Beckleys. The shades were pulled. Marge lit a cigarette. Then she gave her lighter to Tom to light his cigarette. Smoke circled up.

"I've been informed that a possible scandal may erupt over Dave's fight with a black man at the Nahato tavern," Tom said, exhaling smoke. "Not only did he fight with George, he's shown public contempt towards Freddie Toll, the black man on the Giants' team."

"Dave's a town hero," Marge said. "No matter what his bigoted feelings are, he's the hero of the baseball team, and he volunteers to fight fires. He saved Mr. Bartel, remember."

"Yes, I remember," Tom said. "But maybe he's despondent about the ruckus with the black man. Maybe we should arrange a meeting with him."

"I don't see how meeting with him would help," Ridley said. "I propose we try to find someone to run against Jack Mayfield in the November elections. Let's get Mayfield off the city council. With him gone the council would split three to three. At that point, Tom, you'd have the deciding vote."

"Jack's popular too," Marge said. "Who'd vote against him?"

"Well, he's furthering a cause that's dear to him, isn't he?" Ridley said. "He shouldn't be holding that office. He's got too

111

much to lose if the stadium is demolished. He's trying to save his family name. That's a conflict of interest."

"How about this," Arthur said. "Marge, you arrange a meeting with Dave. Let's find out what he's thinking. Tom, you pursue the city council issue and find someone to replace Jack. Surely there's someone who will support our plan of converting the stadium to commercial property. Find that person. I'll covertly finance his campaign."

"I think I know of someone," Tom said. "I'll feel him out."

"Good," Arthur said. "When you've settled on the candidate tell Ridley. Ridley, you start gathering signatures supporting a recall of Jack because of his conflict of interest. Jack will have this scandal to deal with, and it just might eliminate him from contention in the November election." Arthur looked at Marge.

"Tonight's a perfect opportunity for you to meet Dave" Arthur said. "We'll go to the game. When the game's over I'll head for home while you go out on the field to ask for his autograph. Get acquainted. Ask him over for a drink. Tell him I'd like to talk with him. Tell him we're having a party. We'll ask some neighbors over. Maybe Tom and Ridley can come too."

"But I've never been to a baseball game," Marge said.

"Well, tell Dave that," Arthur said.

"Do you think he'd come?"

"He's probably looking for friends right now, Marge," Arthur said. "That mess with the black man, you know. He'll come. Just tell him we'll help him with money or whatever he needs. If he had money he might leave town and try out for the major leagues. Let him know that we're here to help. The paper says the team is built around him. The fans come to the game just to watch him play. If he leaves the team, then the Giants will lose games, and fan support will drop off. With him gone it might provide the opening we've been looking for."

Chapter 29

Just before the big game with Portland, Freddie Toll got a phone call.

"Mr. Toll, my name is Grace Brown. I'm George Brown's wife."

"Yes," Freddie said. "I've been reading the papers about your husband."

"It's very important that I talk with you. Can you come over? I live on the northeast corner of Oak and 5th Street."

"Yes. I'll have to call my manager and tell him I'll be late. After that I'll be right over."

Freddie walked up the stone walkway to Mrs. Brown's small cottage. The yard was neatly kept and the small house had recently been painted. Freddie knocked on the door. Mrs. Brown was about fifty years old and wore a yellow scarf on her head. She was slender and much shorter than Freddie. Freddie ducked past the doorway and into the front room. The lacy curtains were pulled to the side. A well used couch and two chairs filled the small room. Cloth covers hid holes in the ragged upholstery.

"Please have a seat," Grace said. "Would you like something to drink? Coffee, water?"

"No, thank you, Mrs. Brown. Why did you want to talk to me?"

"About George," Grace said. "We've lived here in Greenville for the past five years. Other than one disorderly conduct citation against George it's been relatively peaceful here. Even that charge was bogus. He works hard to provide me with a home. Mostly day labor jobs. It's hard work. Mr. Toll, I know George better than anyone in the world. I know for a fact that he'd never set a fire like they're accusing him of!" She held her head in her hands and began to cry. "But there's no way I can prove it. He's never done a mean thing in his life. He's just that way, very even tempered and not cruel at all." She looked up. "How do I let people know George is a good man? I was hoping you might help us. I thought with your reputation as a baseball star you might have some connections." Grace pulled a handkerchief from her pocket to wipe the tears from her eyes.

"I don't know many people here," Freddie said. "But I'll do what I can." There was no doubt or wavering in Freddie's voice. Two times he'd been picked up by police in San Diego for crimes he hadn't committed. If it hadn't been for his mother he might still be in jail. So he could understand what George was going through. If he was falsely accused then something had to be done. Even though the evidence appeared overwhelming, Freddie knew that George still had to be given a fair break. The only way to give him a chance would be to find a lawyer to represent him. "I'll start looking for an attorney. In the meantime, you call the NAACP and ask them for help."

Back at Jack's, Freddie spent the rest of the evening on the phone. Through the few connections Freddie had, he was able to come to a decision. One lawyer who'd have the best chance of saving George was Virgil Nesting, a Nez Perce Indian with outstanding credentials.

Chapter 30

While Freddie was at George Brown's house trying to figure out a way to help him, Jack and Anne were driving to the baseball game. The big game promised to be a thrilling spectacle—the first in a series of five between the Portland Ravens and the Greenville Giants. The winner of this important series might well be the team winning the pennant at the end of the season.

Jack and Anne sat together in the reserved seating section behind home plate. Anne wore a tight-fitting green silky blouse with a black skirt. Her brown hair was tightly curled. Jack was casually dressed in a white shirt and tan slacks. Jack loved Anne's perfume, never overwhelming, yet wonderfully appealing. He looked over at Anne who was intently watching the players warm up on the field. Jack felt honored to be with her in his grandfather's stadium, watching a team that he and Burt had put together. Jack smiled as he reflected that this was the great thing about baseball, when the Greenville Giants, a team of rejects, could rise above supposed limitations and threaten champions.

Fans crammed into the stadium, jostling against one another, eating hot dogs, and drinking beer. Their team was a success, Jack thought. He couldn't believe it. The team had three of the best players in the Pacific North League. To be enjoying this spectacle with the woman he loved, well it just made him proud.

The Giants were warming up on the field. Macomb warmed up on the mound while the team practiced fielding. Jack saw

Anne's brow tighten as she watched Dave warming up on first base. His nose still sported a small bandage.

"Where's Freddie?" Anne asked.

"I don't know. He's usually the first one on the field."

"I thought Dave was pitching," Anne said.

"At the last minute Burt decided to use Richard," Jack said. "That buzz-ball of his is hard to hit, you know."

"He better be his best tonight," Anne said.

"What do you mean?"

"The Ravens have a famous pitcher, a former Yankee, who's trying to make a comeback. With the Yankees, he threw two shut-outs. The Ravens think he's unstoppable in this league."

"We'll see about that," Jack said.

Over the PA system came, "Replacing Freddie Toll in center field for the giants will be Terrance Bingham."

Both Jack and Anne looked at each other in surprise. "This is news to me," Jack said. "Our chances of winning just dropped a notch."

Then came another announcement: "Tonight the Ravens have Patrick Merick pitching for them." The crowd let out a loud roar of approval and clapped loudly. Jack thought it would be a thrill to see this great man in action.

"He's a clever pitcher," Anne said. "He can't throw his fastball like he once could so now he relies on his change ups and a slower fastball with a last-second curve. After the game I must interview him."

Jack and Anne stood along with the crowd. The players proudly stood with hats off on the baselines. Then a small skinny girl belted out the National Anthem. Loud applause followed.

"Beautiful," Anne said when it was finished. Players jogged onto the field, and a batter warmed up in the batter's circle.

The umpire dusted off home plate and lowered his facemask.

"Play ball!"

Merick was the first to bat for the Ravens. He settled himself into the batter's box. He glared at Macomb. Macomb slung his buzz-ball. It sped past Merick.

"Strike one."

Merick looked back at Burt. "What the hell was that?"

Burt smiled, still crouching. "The buzz-ball."

The next pitch was Macomb's other specialty, a curve ball. Merick couldn't help himself and instinctively swung, hitting air.

"Strike two."

The last pitch was a fastball that made Merick look like a wooden statue.

"Strike three."

Merick bowed to Macomb as he made his way to the dugout. "Buzz-ball? That kid has class," Jack heard him say. Two more outs followed quickly. The Ravens took the field. Merick warmed up.

"Play ball," said the umpire.

"Richard's coming to bat," Jack said. Merick couldn't get him out. Richard fouled everything, low balls, inside curves, knuckle balls, until finally Merick walked him. Gifford came to bat. Gifford tried to bunt but missed the pitched ball.

"Oh, look! Richard's stealing second," Anne said. The Raven's catcher, Dan Stultz, threw to second and the ball sailed over his head. Richard ran to third. Then Merick struck out Gifford, followed by Stewart, and Dave. The inning ended scoreless.

Jack and Anne sat through eight exciting innings. Macomb was close to pitching a shut out. The Giants had managed to get men on base, and Dave had hit three singles and stolen two bases. Yet when the last inning crept up, after many questionable calls from the umpires, the score was still tied at zero to zero. Richard had allowed just four hits. He had struck out seven batters. His buzz-ball was working. Merick was still pitching too, and throwing a great game. Portland came to bat. Richard immediately struck out Bud Cordon, to the cheers of the fans. Pete Gussy hit a sizzling grounder towards third base. Gifford snagged it, and threw the ball to Dave at first.

"You're out!" cried the umpire.

Zorr rushed out to the first base umpire and stood nose to nose with him. "You son of a bitch, you're off the mark. Gussy was safe."

"Not the way I saw it. Gussy was out."

"He was safe! Anyone with eyes could see that," Zorr complained as he walked back to the dugout throwing up his hands.

Merick was the next batter.

"He can hit," Anne said. The first pitch was a fastball. Merick connected with it. The ball soared to the left-center field fence and smacked it high. It bounced back onto the field. Left fielder Duane Wilson and Terrance Bingham collided while trying to pick it up, allowing Merick to make third base. The Ravens' next batter was Ted Peck.

"Peck's their best hitter," Anne said.

Richard began by throwing his famous buzz-ball—two pitches, two strikes. Zorr raced over to the umpire. Jack could hear him chewing the umpire out. But it wasn't that he contested the call, it was about Richard's pitch. Jack heard him yell at the umpire.

"There's something on that ball! Baseballs don't jump around like that."

The umpire held up his hand. "Time out. Let me see the ball." Richard tossed the ball to Burt at home plate. Burt gave the ball to the umpire. He inspected the ball, and then he handed it to Zorr.

"Something funny is going on here," Zorr complained, looking at the ball.

"Looks OK to me," said the umpire. "Play ball!"

Jack watched Richard's next pitch. The ball corkscrewed towards home and actually gained momentum when it ripped past Peck.

"Strike three," called the umpire.

Jack saw Peck scratch his head and walk from the plate.

The crowd roared. Three outs and the Giants came to bat in the bottom of the ninth. Dave was the first batter to face Merrick. As he walked to the plate, the team was yelling at him to get a hit.

Burt gave his hit away signal. "Let's win this one for Richard."

Dave hit Merick's first pitch, sending it soaring over the right field fence. The crowd roared as Dave circled the bases. The team gathered at home plate and pounded Dave on the shoulders as he ran past. The Giants had just won the first of a five-game series. Dave was a hero, but so was Richard for throwing a shutout.

All the celebrating left Jack smiling. What a game, he thought. Before leaving he noticed Arthur and Marge Beckley in the stands. He pointed them out to Anne. "I've never seen them at a game before."

"That's odd," Anne said.

Chapter 31

When the game ended, Marge and Arthur parted. While he walked home, it was Marge's assignment to get Dave's autograph and invite him to their small gathering. One thing she hadn't mentioned to Arthur was that she had enjoyed watching the game. It was the first baseball game of her life. It had been thrilling. She loved the competition. It wasn't brutal like football, yet there was an intensity and danger to the game. She'd been close enough to the field to see the pitchers' fastballs zoom across home plate. She'd wondered if she'd have had the nerve to stand there. Trying to hit a speeding meteorite would not be easy. When hit, the baseballs zoomed across the field like howitzer shells. When the ballplayer fielded it she flinched. She was beginning to be intrigued by this sport.

But now, she had to find her way to the ballfield where the players were signing autographs. She noticed a young man helping out on the field.

"Would you show me how to get out to the field, young man?"

"Follow me," Mike said. He walked along the edge of the grandstand towards the entrance gate. "Over there," Mike pointed.

Marge was wearing casual slacks, with a green-and-white windbreaker. She said, "I want to get Dave Summers' and Patrick Merick's autographs. Can you help me?"

"Sure can," Mike said. "I want to get Merick's too. Follow me."

Marge and Arthur had no children of their own, and frankly

children were a bother to both of them. Yet here was this lad kindly helping her. The usually dour Marge was warming to this child. He was taking time away from his bat boy duties to help her.

"Which one is Patrick?" Marge said.

"He's over there by home plate," Mike said with a baseball in his gloved hand.

Marge trailed behind Mike and got into line. She'd never done anything like this before in her life. But this pitcher had captured her imagination. The way he threw that baseball was incredible. She had to meet him. She and Arthur had never really experienced a baseball game. They had only seen the littering, the parking in their driveway, the blinding stadium lights, the loud cheering crowds. But down here with the fans and watching a game, it was different. She saw the overjoyed faces of children and heard their screams of, "I got his autograph!" Marge thought how the adults acted like kids too, while trying to meet a baseball player. It was all new to her, and frankly was wonderful.

"Hi, young man," Merick said to Mike. "You're wearing the wrong cap." Mike wore a Los Angeles Dodger's cap. "Here, take a cap from the team I love, the Yankees." He signed the cap and gave it to Mike. Then he signed Mike's baseball too. He patted Mike on the head and gave him a friendly wink. "Thanks for your help on the field today."

"Wow!" Mike said as he walked off, admiring his new cap.

Marge found herself face to face with Merick. There were about twenty people lined up behind her. Merick's eyes connected with hers. His were iridescent blue, sparkling with life. He was handsome and about thirty-five years old. Marge could remember when she first met Arthur and how she had felt attracted to him. Locks of curling red hair spilled out from under his cap. With his pin-striped uniform and his baseball cap tilted back, there was a magnetism about this man that left Marge speechless. When he smiled at Marge she almost dropped her program, the very program she wanted him to sign.

"I told the reporters we'd win this game," Merick said to Marge. "I guess I was wrong!"

"Win some, lose some," Marge said a little flustered.

"Give me your program and I'll sign it for you."

"Oh yes, please do," Marge said.

Merick signed Marge's program. "There, you know I don't do this for everyone, I want to give you a special gift. What's your name?"

"Marge," Marge said. "But why me?"

Then Marge watched as the great athlete wrote a special note to her, on a Yankee's cap. Then he presented it to Marge.

"Thank you," Marge said. What did he write, she thought? She worked her way out of the crowd. When she reached the stadium wall, she looked at the cap.

"To Marge, You look new to the sport. Thanks for coming tonight. I hope you'll enjoy many more games."

I wonder how he knew that, she thought. Okay, now I have to find Dave Summers. She looked around and saw another man signing autographs at first base. He looked like the first baseman she'd seen in the game so she walked over and got in line. About ten people waited in front of her. The line whittled down to one.

"I hope you'll last out the season," the man ahead of her said. "We really enjoy watching you play and the team needs you."

"The majors haven't signed me yet." Dave said. "I'll be here until they do." Dave smiled and signed the man's baseball card.

It was Marge's turn. She held out her program. She was feeling like a pro by this time.

"Please sign here," Marge said, pointing to Dave's name on the program. Dave signed it. "One other thing," she said. "My husband and I are interested in your career. We'd like to help you out. We're having a little get together this evening. We live on University Hill. You can see our house from here. It's the green one just above the roof of the stadium, on Olive Street. Could you come?"

"Sure, give me time to finish these autographs and take a shower."

Marge walked to the edge of the field near the exit gate. She happened to look back and saw Mike running out of the team's dressing room lugging a brown bag full bats. Mike looked in her direction and waved. Marge waved back.

Chapter 32

After the game, Jack and Anne went to the Greenville Hotel. They settled into a booth in the lounge. Jack ordered a glass of merlot. Anne had a glass of chablis.

"Hey, how about that Dave Summers," a familiar voice sounded above the lounge music. Robert Moore and his wife stood at their booth.

"Dave and Richard won the game for us," Jack said, as the waitress served the wine.

"We've had a great year," Robert said. "What's this I hear about Dave being subpoenaed in the Nahato fire?"

"He was involved in a fight with George Brown, the black man who set the fire."

"I hope Dave doesn't let it get to him. I don't want him to lose his concentration. We have a shot at the pennant this year."

"Don't forget we have two other great players, Richard and Freddie."

"Where was Freddie tonight?" Robert asked.

"If I know Freddie, he was probably doing something to help George Brown. That's the only thing that would have kept him from playing."

"Anne, I'd like you to meet my office manager, Robert Moore, and his wife, Mindy."

"I've heard so much about you, Robert," Anne said. "Jack says you're a top real estate negotiator. Won't you join us?"

"We just stopped by to say hello," Robert said. "Our baby sitter waits. Nice to finally meet you, Anne. Jack can't keep from talking about you either, and when he stares out the window—oh, well you know." Anne's cheeks reddened. "So long for now. See you in the office tomorrow."

"Bright and early," Jack said.

"Absolutely," Robert replied, and they walked off.

When they left Jack could hear soft classical music coming from an overhead speaker. Jack looked fondly at Anne. Wow, he thought—what a great evening. He thought back on how Anne's soft voice turned almost angry when she'd yell support for the Giants at the game. Good hit! Keep it up! Go, Go Go! Put him out! He loved her enthusiasm. He thought about the times they'd been together—at the Junction City game, at Jerry's Café, at the University Hill house, and at the stadium. She felt more like family than any woman he'd ever dated. Yet tonight she seemed distant. He wondered why. Jack tasted his wine. The thick, hearty merlot warmed his throat and stomach. He raised his eyebrows and looked into Anne's eyes.

"Everything that's happening right now has me uneasy," Anne said.

"I know," Jack said. "If only we could look into the future. Oh, speaking of trouble, here comes the mayor."

"What's this, a victory drink?"

"You could call it that," Jack said.

"The Giants are setting the stage for a pennant series if they keep winning."

"The stage is already set. Even if they lose all of the remaining games they've won the right to play. I never thought it would happen."

"I didn't either. It still doesn't change much. I think the city is being ripped off, by not being able to sell that land. The city would come out ahead if the property were developed. With taxes and all, you know."

"The city will come out ahead by keeping the stadium, and professional baseball. Maybe not monetarily, but the citizens will have a deeper sense of purpose if the historic game of baseball is allowed to continue. The bottom line is not always money."

"Oh, but it is, especially for the financial health of this community. It's my job to promote a healthy economy. The baseball team may be entertaining but it's a bad tradeoff. Let's face it, Jack, you have a vested interest in keeping the stadium. Because of your family heritage, and all."

"If anyone has a vested interest, Mayor, it's you. Your real estate holdings will only become more valuable if the stadium property is developed. My interest is family and community. Your interest is money."

"This conversation is hopeless. I've got to go. There's a party at the Beckleys house. Nice to see you, Anne. See you at the next council meeting, Jack."

"I wonder what they're plotting now?" Jack said as he watched the mayor leave the lounge.

"I don't think there's anything they can do this late in the baseball season."

"You're right, he can't spoil this season. I'm afraid he's thinking about when the season's over. Let's not talk about the mayor, I want to talk about us. One thing I know for sure is that I really enjoyed this evening."

"Me too," Anne said. "I look forward to more evenings like this."

Chapter 33

Marge heard the clink of wine glasses and voices. Three couples had come, plus Ridley and Tom. She'd hired a caterer to bring hors d'oeuvres. She'd emptied her cupboards of booze: whiskey, rum, scotch, and wine. The bottles stood on her kitchen counter. She let her friends help themselves. Two ladies sat on the couch. They leisurely smoked and sipped their drinks. Their husbands stood at the front window next to Arthur and Marge, drinking from their glasses. They all looked down at the roof of the stadium.

"I wonder if we'll ever get the city council to tear down that stadium," Frank Jones said to Arthur.

"Not soon, I'm afraid," Arthur said. "If the team keeps winning the council may never tear it down."

"I see what you mean. Tonight's game sent Janice reeling. She hates it when they win. That's when the noise is loudest and it drives Janice nuts. Honestly Arthur, we're thinking of moving to find a quieter part of town, or a town with a more responsive city council."

"I hope you don't move, Frank. We'll need your support to get the stadium razed."

"You've got our support," Frank said, taking a sip of whiskey.

Ted Parsons agreed. "The sooner we get the stadium out of here the sooner we'll be able to enjoy our neighborhood. Keep me informed on your progress, Arthur. We're eager to help."

Marge looked out the window at the city lights blinking in

the east hills. She hardly heard her neighbor's comments about Greenville's stadium. Something had happened to Marge. She was not dead-set against a baseball stadium anymore. She'd had a delightful time at the ball game, meeting the bat boy and the famous pitcher, and watching an exciting game. She'd never tell Arthur that. He'd think she was crazy. Baseball, he'd say, is the dullest sport ever devised by man. She knew she couldn't change his mind. Or change the direction Arthur, Ridley, and Tom were all heading. Arthur was the leading force in her life. She loved Arthur above everything else. Her life hadn't really started until she married him. His brilliance in business affairs had led to what they now had. Arthur had simply always been right. She respected him immensely. Yet a subtle shift was taking place in Marge's thinking. Why was baseball so bad! She decided to quit thinking about it. She would have to learn to stifle her new feelings towards the game of baseball.

"Well, did you ask Dave to come over tonight?" Arthur asked. "And why are you wearing that silly baseball cap? Take it off!"

"I'd forgotten I had it on." Marge tossed it on the couch next to her neighbor, Janice Jones. "Dave said he'd come. He should be here any minute."

"Marge, your cap is signed by Merick," Janice said. "Did you know he's famous?"

"No."

"He's written books. He'll end up in the baseball hall of fame. This cap is quite a keepsake, especially with the nice inscription he wrote you. Keep it, you won't be sorry."

Marge blushed and looked away from Arthur. Then Marge explained how she had gotten the famous man to sign it. "I think he realized my clumsiness out there, that's why the inscription. He was such a handsome gentleman."

When the doorbell sounded, Mr. Billings answered the door. In walked Dave Summers. Heads turned.

"Thank you for coming, Mr. Summers," Marge said. "This may be a hostile crowd, I'm afraid."

"Really? Maybe I should leave," Dave said, smiling.

"Of course not," Marge said. "These people admire your baseball skills. They just don't appreciate the game being played in their neighborhood."

"Oh yes," Dave said. "I've heard of the University Hill neighbors' complaints. Do you feel that way?"

"Hmm, I'm afraid so," Marge said. "Her hesitation caused Arthur to look her way. She quickly followed up with, "My husband thinks the stadium should come down."

"The effort to tear down the stadium has created quite a stir with local baseball promoters," Dave said.

"Well, we have legitimate concerns. We hope the city council will act responsibly. I want you to meet my husband." Marge led Dave over to Arthur, who stood by the window.

"This is my husband, Arthur," Marge said.

"That was some hit," Arthur said.

"Thanks."

"How does it feel to win a game like that?"

"One step closer to the major leagues."

"Would you like a drink?" Arthur said

"Yes, a bottle of beer would be fine."

"Come with me," Arthur said. He and Marge led Dave to the kitchen. From the refrigerator Marge took out a bottle of beer. She opened it and handed it to Dave.

"What are the chances the major leagues will sign you?" Arthur asked.

"I'm expecting it to happen any day now," Dave said.

"What can I do to help you?" Arthur said.

"Say a few prayers, yell a little louder, I don't know."

"I mean can I help you out financially to get picked up by the majors?"

"Maybe," Dave said, "I'll get back to you on that, okay?"

"Sure," Arthur said with a smile. "What about this matter with the black man, George? The man you fought with at the Nahato tavern?"

"Well, it looks like I may get dragged into court to testify," Dave said. "Hell, all I did was fight with the man. I didn't suspect he'd set fire to the whole damn town."

"That was unfortunate," Arthur said. "Any idea when the trial will take place?"

"Soon, about two weeks, right when the pennant series is being played."

"Dave," Arthur said quietly, "if you need money to leave town in a hurry come and see me. I'm in sympathy with what you did, understand?"

"Yes, I do. You're very generous," Dave smiled.

Marge wasn't in agreement with some things Arthur thought, especially his intolerance on racial matters. But she was willing to put up with some of Arthur's eccentricities. Marge lit a cigarette with her lighter.

"What a flashy lighter," Dave said.

"It was Arthur's gift to me on our fortieth anniversary. I love it."

"Have a cigar?" Arthur offered.

"Yes, thanks," Dave said. He took a cigar. Marge gave him her lighter. It didn't light right off. After a few turns of the flint, the flame snapped upward to the cigar's tip. Dave inhaled, working the cigar between his lips and teeth. At last he let out a puff of blue smoke. The lighter continued to burn.

Marge reached up and flipped the lighter closed.

"Thanks," Dave said.

Ridley and Tom came into the room. Marge introduced them to Dave.

"Do you always play like that?" Ridley said.

"When luck is with me," Dave said, exhaling smoke.

"Tomorrow you get another shot at them, right?" the mayor said.

"T'is true."

"For the hero in a baseball game, you seem sort of down," Tom said.

"You see," Dave said. "I'm not dating anyone right now, and I'd like to find a woman, a companion. You know."

"I saw Jack Mayfield with Anne in the stands tonight," Arthur said. "Didn't you and Anne used to date?"

"Yes, but that's in the past now."

"How do you get along with Jack Mayfield?" Arthur asked.

"Right now he's making money because of me. And to think he tried to kick me off the team! I think he's an asshole. If I were to meet him in a dark alley he may not come out. He's better off if he stays away from me."

Chapter 34

The Portland Ravens won the four remaining games of the series. One of the major reasons for the Greenville losses was that both Freddie Toll and Dave had slipped into batting slumps. Jack read in the sports column Anne had written that, "They couldn't hit a watermelon if it was teed up in front of them." But the Giants still led in their Eastern Division. Consequently, Jack thought, even if the Giants were to lose all of the next five games with Lewiston, the Giants would still claim the Eastern Division championship. The Ravens had won the Western Division championship. So the Pacific North League pennant series was set for September 6, 7, and 8. The Giants had a day off before the start of their last series.

At his kitchen table, Jack was reading the *Greenville News*. He'd just finished reading an article about the latest developments in the Nahato fire investigation. He'd noticed that the trial was to begin on the sixth of September. Jack put down the paper and poured milk over his Wheaties. He spread butter and jam on his toast. Freddie came into the kitchen. He emptied cereal in a bowl and sat down at the yellow kitchen table. They were facing each other in robes, unshaven, with disheveled hair. They munched crispy flakes. Freddie was deep in thought.

"Coffee?" Jack asked.

"What!" the startled Freddie said. "Oh yes, sorry. I was thinking about George." Jack poured coffee and then returned the pot to the stove.

"What about George?" Jack asked.

"At ten I have an appointment with Virgil Nesting. I found out about Nesting from the local president of the NAACP. Virgil's a Nez Perce Indian. He's also a former professional football player. He's made a lot of money. After his football career he went to law school. He passed the Oregon bar about five years ago. Jack, he's wealthy, doesn't need money. He's very picky about the cases he takes, but has to believe in his client's innocence. Only then will he take on the person as his client.

"At three, I've got an appointment with George Brown at the county jail. I thought I'd ask Mr. Nesting to join me. I met with George's wife recently. She wants me to help him. She thinks that since I'm a prominent local black I might have some influence in getting George good legal counsel. I want to hear George's side of the story. All we read about in the papers is incriminating information against him. His wife has a different version of George's character. She feels George is being railroaded. Would you like to come?"

"Sure," Jack said.

At ten o'clock, Jack found himself in the law office of Virgil Nesting.

"I have an appointment with Mr. Nesting," Freddie said to the secretary.

"I'll let him know you're here," the secretary said. "Please be seated."

A few minutes later the fifty-year-old Virgil came out to greet Freddie and Jack. The lawyer was a tall man, slightly stooped, with graying hair that was swept back in a short pony tail. He was over six feet tall and had light brown skin. He sported a snappy red tie. He was genuinely glad to make their acquaintances, yet a smile seemed foreign to his lips. Virgil ushered the men into his office and shut the door behind them. He took his seat behind a small mahogany desk, lit a cigarette, and looked at the two men seated in front of him.

"I think I know why you're here," Virgil said. "It's about George, right?"

Freddie nodded.

"Yesterday," Virgil continued, "just after you called, the local president of the NAACP called me. He wanted to know if I'd help George, too. He was concerned because he knows George well. Says he'd never have set that fire. So I moved up the appointment with George to eleven. If I am to take this case I want to get on it quick. You understand, we don't have much time to prepare a defense. Would you gentlemen care to come along with me to the jail?"

Both Freddie and Jack responded immediately with "Yes."

The three men walked through the jail's lobby into an ante-room. Here they were frisked. The jailer then led them to a small room with a barred door. The door slid open. When the men entered the room, the door clanged shut behind them. George was sitting at an oval table ringed with chairs. He still carried bruises from the Nahato fight, and he held one arm tightly against his ribs. His head was supported by his other hand. Sunlight peeked through a small high window.

"You look awful," Virgil said.

"I feel awful," George grimaced.

"I may represent you in court," Virgil said. "Your wife is very concerned. I'd like to find out the truth about what happened that night. What were you doing at the lumber mill?"

George lifted his head from his hand and looked directly at Virgil. The pain in George's eyes reflected not only his current bruises but also the memory of that night. The two men looked at each other for what seemed a long time.

137

"I went into the tavern," George finally said, "to call my wife so she could bring me some gas." George's voice grew stronger. "My car was parked alongside the highway about a block from the tavern. I saw that sign above the door, 'No Niggers' but there wasn't any other place to go. I knew I shouldn't go in there. But I needed gas. So I went inside. That's when all hell broke loose. They wouldn't let me outta that place unless I fought with that baseball player."

"Slow down," Virgil said. "What exactly do you mean, they wouldn't let you out of that place?"

"First they said their phone was out of order," George said. "Then the bartender told me to leave. I backed for the door and someone tripped me. Before I knew it the crowd was yelling for a fight. That's when the baseball player stepped out of the crowd, wanting to fight me."

"That baseball player," Virgil said. "Who are you talking about?"

"Dave Summers," George said. "He wanted to fight me. So the crowd drug me out into the parking lot. I told them I didn't want to fight."

"That's outrageous," Virgil said standing up. "Those devils. What happened next?"

"They forced me to fight. I not only fought with Dave, but when I got too close to the crowd they'd punch me too."

"Those bastards!" Virgil said looking down on George. "Go on."

"The next thing I remember is waking up in the parking lot. I'd lost some teeth, and my ribs ached something fierce. I knew I had to get out of there fast. So I stumbled back to my car and got my gas can. Then I walked over to the mill."

"Did anyone see you with the gas can?"

"I can't be sure. The investigator claims there are witnesses saying I had a gas can. Anyway I found the gas pump and it was unlocked. But I was really scared. So while keeping alert for a

138

night watchman, I tried to operate the pump. As I fumbled with the gas hose, trying to fill the can, I spilled some gas on myself. I stumbled back to my car and put the gas in the tank."

"Did anyone see you on your way back to your car?"

"I don't know. After filling the tank I drove home."

"What time did you get home?'

"I'm not sure. Halfway there I stopped and slept until about four or five in the morning. When I woke up I could barely move, but I still managed to drive home. Jane was still up. She was worried sick about me."

"Who's Jane?"

"My wife," George said. "She called Dr. Ferguson. He came right over. He said I'd lost three front teeth and had two cracked ribs. I swear to you sir, I had nothing to do with that fire. Somebody's trying to frame me."

"I believe you, George," Virgil said. "One problem is that you don't have an alibi. Since you were asleep, there's no one to vouch for you during the time the fire was set. You probably were unconscious because of your wounds. You didn't deserve that beating. I'm appalled at what these men did to you. I'm taking your case. Believe me, we'll try to get you out of here."

Chapter 35

Marge sat on her blue couch reading the morning paper. She put her coffee cup down and lit a cigarette. After reading the national news she read the city news. George Brown's trial was coming soon. The paper's review revealed nothing new. Twenty people were ready to testify against George, placing him right at the scene of the crime. The fact that he'd been beaten up just before the fire supplied the motive. She was convinced he'd done it. Simple revenge. I would have done it myself, she thought.

She adjusted her red robe before reading the sports pages. Ever since the baseball game she'd followed the progress of the Giants and Ravens in the Pacific North League. She thought it funny that a person, 62 years old, could all of a sudden get so excited about the sport of baseball. Yet here she was reading about the teams and hoping she might meet the Raven's pitcher, Merick, one more time.

It looked as though she might get that opportunity. She read that the season was winding down. After taking three of five games in their last series the Giants won the East Division outright. Freddie Toll and Dave were still experiencing terrible batting slumps but the team had managed to squeak past Lewiston. Dave's pitching was suffering, too. If it hadn't been for Macomb's pitching, the Giants would not have finished the season so strong. Anne's newspaper column reported that Burt was seriously considering replacing Dave at first base with Rudy. Rudy was a good hitter.

Maybe his slump could be attributed to the upcoming trial, Marge thought. She could understand that. Dave's name kept coming up in the news, the poor man. He had a lot on his mind—the upcoming pennant series and the big trial. Secretly, Marge looked forward to the Pacific North League playoff series. It was early September. The best two-out-of-three games would decide the league championship. The first game would be played at Greenville's historic Civic Stadium. Marge wished Arthur wanted to go.

Marge thought it was a strange coincidence that the series opened on a Monday night, the same day the trial of George Brown was scheduled to begin.

Arthur stooped as he came through the arched opening into the living room. He held his brown robe tightly around his body. He was coughing and pale. He'd developed a cough two weeks ago.

"Arthur, you should go to the doctor!" Marge said. "You coughed all night."

"I think I will," Arthur said wearily, and blew his nose into a tissue. "My throat's terribly sore, and I had a hard time breathing last night."

"Why wait any longer. Let's go now." Marge threw the paper on the couch. "I'm taking you to the emergency room. Get dressed."

Marge waited outside the emergency room as Dr. Jacobs examined Arthur. It must have been a half hour before the doctor retuned.

"I'm afraid Arthur has a case of pneumonia," Dr. Jacobs said. "He'll have to remain at the hospital so we can keep an eye on him." Marge stayed the rest of the day. Arthur continued to get worse.

"We have a bed down the hall if you get tired," the nurse said. When Arthur dozed off, Marge found the bed, laid down, and dropped off into a restless sleep.

"Mrs. Beckley!" the nurse shook Marge's shoulder.

"What is it?" Marge said struggling to get up.

"I'm very sorry."

"No!"

"I'm afraid so," The nurse said. "We were going to come and get you but there wasn't time. He died a few minutes ago. We did everything we could to save him. Nothing worked. He's gone. "

Marge sobbed quietly as she sat on the edge of the bed. The nurse sat next to Marge and put her arm around her.

The next morning Marge sat alone on her couch, whimpering and gazing at the hills and clouds to the east. It looked like rain. Bouquets of flowers adorned her mantle and were strewn on her living room carpet. Attached were stupid bereavement cards. As if her loss of Arthur could be explained in prose. Arthur had meant everything to her. She felt an emptiness like nothing she'd ever felt before. She hadn't slept and her eyes were red. Two unread copies of the *Greenville News* and soggy tissues lay next to her.

Her phone rang. Marge let it ring. After five rings it stopped. Thirty minutes later it rang again.

"Hello," Marge said.

"Good morning," the booming voice of the mayor said. "Ridley is here and we want you to know how sorry we are. If there is anything we can do, please call."

"Thank you," Marge said. "Right now I want to be left alone."

"Right," the mayor said. "However we still have this matter of the stadium confronting us. I've been encouraging Wes Lathum to run against Mayfield for a seat on the city council. The elections are in November so we can't waste a minute. Ridley has circulated petitions showing that Mayfield has a conflict of interest by trying to save the stadium. The petitions have raised enough controversy that Jack's try for reelection will be threatened. Now we need money to help fund Wes's campaign. Arthur had promised to help at our last meeting. I know this is not the time to ask, but we need some of that money to get the campaign off the ground."

"I remember him saying that," Marge said. "But I feel differently now."

"What? You can't back out now. We've done everything just like Arthur wanted."

Marge hung up. The phone rang again. Marge didn't answer.

Chapter 36

Two days later, Dave rang Marge's doorbell. He waited with a big bouquet of roses in his hand. He saw the large peephole open and Marge's eyes looking at him. The door opened slowly.

"I heard of Arthur's death," Dave said. "So I brought you some flowers. Can I do anything to help?"

"No," Marge said sadly. "Let me find a vase for those beautiful roses. I'll probably have to put them in the sink for now; I've run out of vases. Please come in. Would you like some coffee?"

"Yes," Dave said, as he walked over the threshold down the hall and into Marge's front room. He took the big cushioned chair that faced the couch. He watched as Marge walked into the kitchen which adjoined the living room. She was wearing her red bathrobe with a white sash around her waist. Her eyes were red and she blew her nose often.

"Please excuse my robe. I just haven't felt like dressing today. I'm usually much tidier," Marge said.

"I understand completely."

"Would instant coffee be all right?"

"Perfect," Dave said. Dave saw the gold lighter on the coffee table. He reached down and examined the inscription. After reading it he sat the lighter back down. Marge walked back into the room. She picked up her fabric covered cigarette box took out a cigarette and lit it.

"Would you like a cigarette?" she asked, exhaling.

"No thanks," Dave said.

She sat the lighter and cigarettes back on the coffee table and walked back to the kitchen. Dave waited patiently for her to return. When she came through the kitchen door she was carrying two cups of coffee. She gave one to Dave and sat down on the couch.

"I was sad to hear about Arthur's death," Dave said. "I could tell right off that you two had been together for a long time."

"Forty-two years," Marge said. "Everything I have is because of him—our house, car, business holdings, everything. Of course I've helped manage things too. I often felt like his secretary. We worked together well. The stadium is another issue. I think our desire to see it razed was wrong."

"Have you told anyone else this?" Dave asked.

"No," Marge said.

"You mean you like baseball now?" Dave said, questioning Marge's logic.

"Yes. I've been reading the paper, Anne's sports column. She's managed to get me really excited about the upcoming pennant series." Marge snuffed out her cigarette.

She picked out another and lit it.

This new information surprised Dave. "Are you going to the games?"

"Sure," Marge said. "You know I think the games will help me get my mind off of Arthur. And I'm looking forward to seeing you play."

Dave couldn't believe what he was hearing. He'd felt so sure he'd be able to get some money from her, since Arthur had told him if he needed money to come to him. But Arthur had died. Marge was different. "I may not be playing in the opener."

"I'm sorry to hear that," Marge said. "Why not?"

"I'm in a batting slump and can't seem to pull out of it. I've spent long hours practicing, trying to improve. Nothing is doing any good. I think Jack Mayfield wants me benched. Then there's

George Brown's trial."

"You poor man. Do you think George is guilty of setting the mill on fire?" Marge asked.

"Yes," Dave said. "He got a little roughed up at the tavern. The fire was his way of getting revenge. It's really got me upset. Yesterday I was slapped with a subpoena to testify. All these factors are affecting my batting. That's the reason I'm here. Arthur offered me some money if I'd leave town, to go and try out for the major leagues. I'm thinking of doing that when the pennant series is over. You know, he agreed with me that I'd done the right thing. Now I'm here for the money he offered."

"You're the second person to ask me for money," Marge said. "I need some time. I'm also under stress. Surely you can understand."

"Oh yes, I know. Life has thrown you a curveball."

"You must also understand that I'm not responsible for decisions Arthur made about giving out money. Plus I don't agree with all of his views, especially when it comes to intolerance. I've read in the paper about how you beat up George. You must have been forced into it, right?" Marge said.

"I had to do it," Dave said.

"Unfortunately, Arthur was a racist." Marge said. "Not many people knew. Are you a racist, Dave?" Just then the phone rang. "Hello? Oh, yes, Tom, what is it?" With her hand over the receiver she whispered to Dave "It's the mayor. I'll be right back." She walked to the kitchen extension, and closed the door.

Dave didn't like her nosy questions. Marge reentered the room to hang up the living room extension, and then returned to the kitchen. Dave was getting antsy. Finally he decided to leave. He gently knocked on the kitchen door. She opened it a crack.

"Yes,"

"I have to go, we'll talk later," Dave said.

"Bye," Marge said.

Maybe I can get some money from the mayor, Dave thought.

It was 5 p.m. when Dave reached Greenville's City Hall. When he walked into the office the secretary was on the phone. She motioned him to take a seat. When she hung up she asked "Do you have an appointment?"

"No," Dave said. "I'd like to talk with the mayor if he's available."

"Your name, sir?"

"Dave Summers."

"Dave Summers, the baseball star?"

"Yes."

The secretary raised her eyebrows. "Go right in, Mr. Summers. The mayor's office is the first door on the right. He's with Ridley at the moment, but I think they'll want to meet you."

"Thanks," Dave entered the mayor's office, and closed the door behind him. Ridley and the mayor rose to shake Dave's hand. Then Ridley sat down on the couch. The mayor backed into his swivel chair. Dave saw a smile break on his lips. Dave took the chair in front of the mayor's desk.

"What brings you here?" Tom asked, leaning back.

"I'm here because of Arthur. He was willing to lend me money to get out of town. George Brown's lawyer, Virgil Nesting, is building a case around George that's making me look like the bad guy. I don't want to stay in this town under those circumstances. You understand, don't you?"

"Yes," said the mayor, winking at Ridley. "We might be able to help you. How much will you need?"

"Five thousand," Dave said.

"How about if we give you half now, and the rest when the series is over?" Ridley suggested.

"Why?"

148

"You know why," the mayor said.

"I see," Dave responded. "You want me to throw the series."

"We didn't say that," Ridley said. "But if the Giants just happened to lose then there'd be another twenty five-hundred dollars for you."

"I can't do that," Dave said.

"Would you promise Ridley and me you'll leave town after the series?"

"Yes," Dave said.

The mayor walked over to a door and opened it. Inside the closet was a floor safe. The mayor swiveled the combination right then left. The door swung open. From a box he withdrew twenty-five hundred dollars. He closed everything up and returned to his chair. Reaching over the desk he offered Dave the money.

"You won't regret this," Dave said. "I'll be gone when the season ends, you can count on it."

Chapter 37

It was two days before the first game of the pennant championships with the Portland Ravens. Burt showed up at Jack's real estate office to discuss strategies for the series.

"Why not replace Dave with Rudy?" Jack said. "Let Dave know he's really helped us, but he's not hitting right now. He should understand that."

"I've seriously considered it," Burt said. "Everything that's happening in Dave's personal life is affecting his game. He really resents that Anne is dating you. That man does not like to lose anything. He doesn't spare words about you, either. If I hear anymore of his wisecracks he'll be on the bench for good."

"It's about time he got over losing Anne," Jack said. "She wants nothing to do with him. Even her articles about his baseball exploits are strained. Fortunately, she hasn't had to write much about him lately. His hitting slump, you know. But I'm glad about one thing. I'm glad his hate is directed at me and not Anne."

"Yes, but be warned, stay away from him," Burt said. "The other thing that bothers him is that Freddie Toll is becoming a leader of the team. Freddie's making up for Dave. He doesn't like being shown up by a black man. But that's exactly what's happening. Freddie's batting slump will end. He's been practicing really hard. I see him hitting in the mornings, taking pitches from Gilroy. The series championship now rests with Freddie getting out of his slump and Macomb's pitching. I haven't given up on Dave, either. He can still help this team.

"It's that damn trial. Why couldn't it have been started after the series? To have it start on the same day as the series opens is tough for Dave. Since Dave's been subpoenaed he's got that on his mind too. Plus George's lawyer, Virgil Nesting, has been trying to get an interview with Dave. Dave has stayed clear of Virgil. That man is one of the shrewdest attorneys in the state. Did you know he's been asked to run for Oregon's attorney general?"

"No," Jack said. "I went with Freddie when Mr. Nesting interviewed George. Virgil really got fired up. He was pretty mad when we left George's cell."

"I'll let Dave know he's out of the lineup for the first game," Burt said. "He's going to be pissed. He'll probably blame it on you. So be careful."

"Thanks for the warning," Jack said. "Freddie and I are going to the trial the day of the game. Freddie may be a little late for the pre-game ceremonies. But I can guarantee you one thing. His enthusiasm for this game is high. He can hardly wait. Even the tension of a championship game hardly fazes him. He's anxious to get on with it."

"That's good," Burt said. "Because there will be major league scouts looking at him. He's sure to be signed. I'll be happy when it happens. Freddie's worked hard. Oh, one other thing. There's a report by a city engineer that a structural member under the south grandstand is weak. It needs reinforcing. We need that fixed pronto, before the first game."

"I'll take care of it," Jack said.

Chapter 38

The day before the opening game of the pennant series, Jack waited in the stadium parking lot for the city engineer. Jack noticed Dave's yellow Cadillac parked at the east end of the parking lot. Why is he here, Jack thought? He made a move to go look in the car, but then the engineer arrived and parked his green Chevy next to Jack's station wagon. Bruce Myers, a man in his forties, climbed out of his car. He was balding, with a double chin and his stomach hung over his belt. He sauntered up to Jack.

"Good morning," Jack said.

"Hi, I'm in sort of a hurry," Bruce said. "I've another appointment right after this."

"Follow me," Jack led Bruce to the south end of the stadium. Jack noticed the door going to the substructure of the stadium standing open. That's odd, he thought. No one is supposed to be in there. They were about to walk through the door when Dave appeared. He was holding a flashlight. When he saw Jack, Dave frowned and was going to pass them by.

"What are you doing here?" Jack asked.

"None of your business!" Dave said. "Get out of my way, or I'll flatten you." He shoved Jack aside and started for the parking lot.

Jack shook his head.

"I must get this inspection done now," Bruce said, "in order to call in the repair."

"Okay," Jack said. "Let's get this job done. I'll deal with Dave later." He knew he'd have to tell Burt what happened.

"It's an easy repair," Bruce said and he showed Jack what needed to be done. "I can have a man on it this afternoon if you give me the OK."

"You got it," Jack said.

Chapter 39

Dave was at home when he got Burt's evening call.

"Hi, Dave," Burt said.

"Hi, coach."

"You're in big trouble, Dave," Burt said. "Why'd you shove Jack?"

"Aw, I was disgusted. I was trying to find a friend's heirloom pen knife. He'd lost it through a crack in the bleachers. I couldn't find it. Then Jack showed up. I guess I blew up. You know how I feel about that asshole."

"If it wasn't for Jack we wouldn't have a team. If it wasn't for you we wouldn't be in the championships. What would you do if you were in my position?"

"I don't know."

"Here's my solution. You're out of the line-up tomorrow night," Burt said. "I'm replacing you at first base with Rudy. If he gets injured then you go in, got it?"

"Yes."

"The other reason for replacing you is the hitting slump you're in. Rudy's hitting good right now."

"Will I be pitching during the series?" Dave asked.

"Yes, but Gilroy will be pitching in the opener."

"My hitting is coming back, I can feel it. I've been practicing."

"I know, I've seen you. But you touch Jack one more time and you're off the team."

The phone went dead.

So I blew up at Jack, so what! Dave thought. Burt knows I don't like the man. Everybody blows a gasket now and then. Burt's wrong in taking me out of tomorrow's game. I can help this team, and he knows it. All players go through slumps. I could break out of it tomorrow night. I'll bet I'm back in the lineup after two innings. That damn Mayfield! He'll stop at nothing until he gets me off the team. I should have flattened him. I don't give a rip anymore. I'm leaving this burg as soon as the season ends and George Brown's trial is over.

Chapter 40

The trial was set to convene on the same day the Pacific North League championship series was to begin. The courtroom was jammed with people—reporters, witnesses, attorneys, and a host of Greenville citizens. George was shackled. He sat with Virgil at a table in front. The prosecution attorney, Walter Paige, sat at a table across from the accused. He was a small, thin man with slicked-down black hair. His mustache and beard were meticulously trimmed. His facial features were unusually small, almost feminine. Twelve jurors sat in the jury box.

From the third row, Jack noticed Dave Summers sitting with witnesses in the front. Sitting next to Jack were Anne and Freddie. The low murmur of indistinct voices filled the courtroom. Jack could almost feel Freddie's concern for George. At home, Freddie talked a lot about how he thought George was innocent.

"Who else could have set that fire?" Freddie had asked. "Maybe a disgruntled mill employee? Was Virgil pursuing that angle?" Virgil had called Freddie earlier and explained that a grand jury had filed an indictment against George because of the overwhelming circumstantial evidence. He'd told Freddie it'd be a difficult case.

Then the bailiff ordered the courtroom quiet.

"Does the prosecution have an opening statement?" Judge Anthony Belton asked.

"Yes, your honor," Walter Paige said, standing. He paced over to the jury. "Ladies and gentlemen of the jury, it has come to our attention that George Brown committed a fiendish act. We will prove that on the night in question, the defendant deliberately set fire to the Nahato Lumber Mill and Tavern. He did this as an act of revenge for being beaten up earlier in the evening. This frightful act resulted in one Sam Taylor being burned to death. There is a preponderance of evidence connecting the defendant with these crimes.

"Mr. Brown was seen by twenty witnesses carrying a gas can to the mill. He cannot account for where he was when the fire was set. Then, when he got back to town about four or five in the morning he was treated for injuries by his doctor. His doctor will testify that the defendant's clothing reeked of gas. This is what you'll have to decide. Did the defendant commit these crimes?"

"Does the defense want to present an opening statement?" Judge Belton asked.

Virgil Nesting stood, "Your honor I'll present my opening statement tomorrow when I present the defendant's case."

"Very well," the Judge said. "The prosecution may continue."

"Our first witness is Larry Bales, proprietor of the Nahato Tavern."

Mr. Bales was sworn in and took the witness stand.

"Mr. Bales, what did you see the night of the fire?" Paige asked.

"George lost a fight in the parking lot of my tavern."

"Who did he fight?"

"Dave Summers."

"How many people witnessed the fight?"

"About twenty of my customers," Larry said.

"Why was the defendant fighting?"

"Aw, we were just having fun," Larry said. "But we got carried away. Dave Summers punched him around pretty good. You know, there's a sign over the front door of my tavern that says 'no niggers.' Dave and the rest of the boys were just enforcing my rules. Of course when the fight started we all cheered Dave along. When George was knocked unconscious that ended the fight. We made sure the defendant was still alive and moved him to a safe spot in the parking lot. I think it was just one of those events where men drank too much."

"Did you and your customers see Mr. Brown carrying his five-gallon gas can towards the mill later that night?"

"Yes, after he gained consciousness he got his gas can. We saw him walk past the front of the tavern. We wondered at the time where he was going. But we didn't do anything. Of course we didn't' think he'd set fire to the mill and my tavern. He tried to kill us!"

The courtroom's audience let out a gasp.

"That's all, Mr. Bales," Paige said.

Jack watched as Virgil and George exchanged notes.

"My next witness is Dr. Ferguson," Paige said. After being sworn in Dr. Ferguson took the stand.

"Dr. Ferguson, did you treat George's wounds the morning of the fire?" Paige asked.

"Yes sir, I did."

"What time was that?"

"About 5:30 am."

"How badly was he injured?"

"He'd lost three front teeth and I detected two cracked ribs."

"Did you smell gasoline on George's clothes?"

"Yes."

"Does the defendant smoke cigarettes?"

"Yes."

That's when Paige looked to the jury. "Ladies and gentlemen of the jury, George Brown not only stole gas from the mill, but he also had the means to ignite it."

Jack and Freddie exchanged questioning looks.

"You may step down. My next witness is fire chief Wilber Caulkins."

Jack saw the chief sworn in and then take the stand.

"Was this fire accidental or deliberate?" Paige asked.

"Deliberate."

"How many gallons of gas would it take to create an inferno of this type?"

"Quite a few. We found some rags that had been doused with gas. We feel certain that this was the way in which the perpetrator destroyed the mill and tavern—strategically placed rags that had been doused in gas. By the time we got there the mill and tavern were practically destroyed. Our job then was to keep the fire from spreading to nearby homes and the forests."

"Where did the rags come from?"

"They were typical of torn-up clothing found in the back seat of George Brown's car."

Anne sighed. "I hadn't heard that before."

"Shhh," Jack said.

"Had the body of Sam Taylor shown any abuse?"

"No," the chief said. "We think he fell asleep on the job. He died of smoke inhalation."

"No more questions, your Honor. My next witness is the Nahato Lumber Mill owner, Mr. Hugh Lofton. Will you please come forward for the oath and take the stand?"

Mr. Lofton walked past Jack with his thumbs around his suspenders.

"Mr. Lofton," Paige said. "From your records, were you able to ascertain how much gas was taken?"

"Yes, about 25 gallons is unaccounted for."

"Do you know of anyone who would want to destroy your

mill? A disgruntled employee, or a rival in the lumber business?"

"We've never laid anyone off, and our employees are fiercely loyal. My competitors are honorable men. I can't think of anyone who would do such a thing."

"Was Sam Taylor a valued employee?"

"One of the best!"

"Where you surprised when you'd found out he'd fallen asleep on the job?"

"You can't work an entire night without dozing off once in a while."

"That's all, Mr. Lofton."

The prosecutor next asked Mr. Tompkins, a fingerprint specialist with the Greenville police department, to take the stand. After Tompkins was sworn in Paige started his questioning.

"Did you examine the Nahato mill gas pump for fingerprints?"

"Yes."

"Did you find the fingerprints of George Brown on that pump?"

"Yes, all over the nozzle, hose, and pump. Plus his prints are on the gas can too."

Anne's elbow whacked Jack's. She leaned over. "It's not looking good for George."

"Virgil said the prosecutor had a good case." Jack said. "So far George's side of the story is being smothered."

"I know," Anne said.

The prosecutor summed up the day's testimony. "Your honor and members of the jury, we have confiscated Mr. Brown's car, rags from his back seat, the gas can, and the clothes he wore that evening. Those items are being held as evidence. We have affidavits from every witness who was at this horrific crime. The evidence shows that when George Brown woke from unconsciousness in the Nahato Tavern parking lot, he went to his car and removed the rags. While the night watchman slept, the defendant

161

carefully placed the rags around the mill and tavern. He returned to his car and got the gas can. Then he deliberately walked back to the mill and stole the mill's gas. Not just five gallons but twenty-five! With the stolen gas he doused the rags. The register on the gas pump survived the fire. It proved how much gas was taken. No one else used gas that night. Mr. Brown says he fell asleep in his car during the time the fire was being set. In other words, he can't verify where he was. Mr. Brown smokes cigarettes, so he could easily have used his matches to ignite the gas. He had more than one motive for this crime. First, he saw the sign over the Tavern's door that denigrates his race. Then he was beaten up in the parking lot."

Paige looked directly at the jurors, "Wouldn't these humiliating events have stirred you to violence? We feel that our case against Mr. Brown shows beyond a reasonable doubt that he is responsible for the fire at the Nahato mill and tavern, and that by these actions he caused the death of Sam Taylor."

Judge Belton ordered the defendant kept in confinement. "The defendant's attorney, Vigil Nesting, will present his case tomorrow at 10 a.m. This court is adjourned."

Chapter 41

Monday night finally came. Jack had worked overtime preparing the opening ceremonies for the first game of the pennant series. He'd tried to talk world-class runner Steve Prefontaine into coming, hoping his presence would bring in more fans. Prefontaine could have thrown the opening pitch in the game had he come. But a conflict with a scheduled track meet made it impossible.

Thus he had to go with his other idea, to buy one hundred green balloons and send them aloft. Mike Ward, the bat boy, was assigned the job of inflating them. They were to be released at exactly 7 pm. Then Barbara Winston, a music student at the university, was to sing the National Anthem, a cappella. As the balloons ascended into the sky the league president, William Axelrod, would make a short address. Then he'd throw out the first pitch. The game would start at 7:10 pm.

Jack and Anne sat behind home plate in the reserved section. The east-facing stadium had filled with fans, and shade dappled them. Jack saw Richard Macomb and Betty Jo sitting higher in the stands. Richard had the night off because he was scheduled to pitch in the second game. A blue-and-white polka-dot sky hung overhead. The sun was dropping fast. The stadium's shadow eased out onto the field. Dignitaries from the league sat in chairs at home plate next to a microphone. The team's players sat in their respective dugouts. The Team managers, Zorr and Andrews, were on the infield shaking hands with the league representatives. Suddenly the brilliant overhead lights bleeped on. Lights on

163

the scoreboard flashed on and off. The league president, William Axelrod, tapped the microphone. "Testing, testing, testing."

I hope everything goes as planned, Jack thought. Anne's attention was riveted on the field. At 7 p.m. the balloons were released. But instead of lifting off the ground and into the air they rolled about on the grass. There wasn't the slightest breeze to provide a lift off. Why weren't those balloons filled with gas? Mike must have used air instead of helium. There's always some hang-up, Jack thought.

A casually-dressed Miss Winston strode up to the mike. The baseball players lined up along the first base and third base lines. The dignitaries stood as a group. All faced the United States flag in center field. Miss Winston then sang an inspiring rendition of the national anthem. The balloons drifted in front of the standing dignitaries. One bumped up against Barbara. Barbara finished her stirring performance. Mike was ordered to corral the balloons and get them off the playing field. The league president addressed the crowd.

"I hope the flightless green balloons are not a bad omen for the Giants this evening," Axelrod said. Snickers and laughs rippled through the crowd. Jack was embarrassed. Anne looked at him and all he could do was shrug. "I want you all to know that by being fans in this important league you are helping young men realize their dreams of playing professional baseball. You are fortunate to have some of the best managers in baseball. Two of these managers, Burt Andrews and Bob Zorr, have led their clubs to division championships. These two clubs will now compete for the Pacific North League pennant. So let's begin."

After the umpire dusted off home plate, he lowered his grilled mask. "Play ball!"

The Giants ran onto the field. The Ravens' batters practiced their swings next to the stands. The chairs and microphone were removed. Mr. Axelrod stood at the pitcher's mound. Then the Giants manager/catcher, Burt Andrews, took his position behind home plate. He raised his mitt. Mr. Axelrod threw the ball. The 1974 Pacific North League championship games were under way.

As the inning began, Jack reminisced. Sitting next to him was the delight of his life. Every day Jack and Anne found something new that they had in common, similar expressions and ideas. Their thoughts about politics, education, and sports coincided. The people she liked, he liked. The only possible thing he found wrong with Anne was her naiveté. She was easily conned by people. She was just too trusting. Take Dave Summers for instance—she was really taken in by him. Regardless, the glint in her blue eyes is what captured Jack's heart. He decided that when he proposed to Anne, he'd do it right here in this stadium.

The first inning ended scoreless. Two more innings passed with no scores. Anne stood up when Freddie came to bat in the bottom of the forth. "Come on, Freddie, get a hit!"

Freddie pounded his bat on home plate, and then turned his eyes toward the pitcher. His body tensed. The pitcher wound up and quickly hurled a fastball. It sped towards Freddie. Freddie swung mightily but missed the ball completely.

Anne's arms flailed, "Hit it Freddie!" Jack had to duck to keep from being smacked. Freddie stepped out of the batter's box. He looked at the third base coach for instructions. Then he stepped back into the box and waited patiently for the next pitch. It was another fastball. Freddie struck air once more. The next pitch bounced in front of home plate.

"Ball one," said the umpire.

Freddie, continuing his slump, struck out. With Freddie's bat quieted and Dave out of the lineup, the Giants had little chance of winning. But Tom Gilroy's pitching was holding the Ravens at bay. He was pitching one of his finest games.

Jack held up a hand to attract the hot dog vendor.

"Would you like a hot dog, or a Coke?" he asked Anne.

"Sure," Anne said. Jack paid for the food, and got a beer for himself.

The fifth inning had just begun, so Anne stood with the food in her hands. "Pitch it in there, Tom!" Juggling the hot dog and the Coke, she dropped some relish on Jack's pants.

"Hey, Anne, watch it!"

"Oh, sorry." She sat down to finish the hot dog.

The first batter, Don Cordon, grounded out to Rudy on first base. The second struck out. It appeared to Jack that Gilroy was going to keep the Ravens scoreless. Then Ted Peck, third base-man for the Ravens, hit a long fly ball that soared to left field. An excited Anne stood again. "Wilson slipped!" she moaned. "He dropped the ball!" Wilson fielded his error and threw the ball to the short stop. Peck tagged up on second base for a double. Anne sat back down. Gilroy's next pitch was a fastball. Pete Gussy hit a grounder to Gifford at third. He picked it up on the first bounce and threw high to Rudy on first base. Anne was on her feet. "The ball went over his head!" By the time Rudy had fielded it, Peck scored and Gussy was on second. Anne was still standing. Jack slowly stood up. Soon they were shouting together, "Put the bums out!" After the trumpet blast they yelled, "Charge!" Hank Cunningham came to bat. He hit the second pitch. It was an in-field pop up. Ben Martin snagged it to retire the side.

Anne looked worried, "The Giants are losing!"

While the Giants scrambled towards their dugout, the Ravens took the field. Jack put his arm around Anne and hugged her. Then he bent down and kissed her. It wasn't a peck on the lips either, but a kiss that might have lasted into the New Year had it not been for nearby fans.

"Sit down in front!"

"Do that at home!"

"I want to see the game!"

"Watch the game for Christ's sake!"

When they sat down, Anne nestled her head on Jack's shoulder.

Even though Gilroy had shut the Ravens down after the fifth innings' disastrous errors, the Giants couldn't mount an offensive. So the Ravens won the game one to nothing.

The Ravens needed just one more game to win the pennant. Because of repairs being made on the Ravens' stadium in Portland the next game would be played in Greenville. If Greenville didn't win, it would be the last.

Chapter 42

Jack and Anne sat outside her apartment in Jack's dark blue station wagon.

"Fred feels bad," Jack said. "He's not hitting, and he strikes out often—too often. The team needs a hitter in there. I've asked Burt to put Dave back in the lineup. It's only a matter of time before Dave starts hitting again. I personally don't like the man. But damn it, he's a good ballplayer."

"What do you think Burt will do?"

"I'm not sure. I told Burt about meeting Dave at the stadium the other morning and how rudely Dave treated me. Thank goodness the engineer was there. I asked Dave what he was doing under the stadium. He said it was none of my business, then pushed me aside. Burt was furious when he found out. He almost kicked Dave off the team."

"Why was Dave there?"

"Burt told me he was looking for a friend's heirloom penknife," Jack said. "The knife had fallen through a crack in the bleachers, I guess. Then Burt told me it would probably be best if I stayed away from him until the season ends. He's probably right. All I know is if the Giants are going to win, we need Dave playing tomorrow night. We'll deal with his unpredictable personality later. I think Burt's going to do it. If he does put Dave back in the lineup then we'll have two good hitters. We'll see what happens."

"I can hardly wait for tomorrow night. Macomb's pitching,

you know. Would you like a glass of wine, Jack?"

"Yes," Jack said.

Inside Anne's apartment, Jack sat on the couch while Anne went to get glasses and the bottle of wine. She put them on the coffee table along with a corkscrew. Jack removed the cork with a pop and poured two glasses of merlot. Anne put some popular LPs on her record player. Her apartment had two bedrooms and a bath upstairs.

"There's a cute veranda off the bedroom," Anne said as she sat down, her head nestling up to Jack's shoulder. "That veranda is why I rented it. There's a great view of Jefferson Butte. I watch the sunrise in the morning and drink coffee. It's very peaceful. To-morrow's going to be a big day, with the trial in the morning and the game at night."

"Are you able to come to the trial?" Jack said.

"Yes," Anne said sipping wine. "I'll meet you and Fred there."

"Virgil Nesting is presenting George's case," Jack said. "Should be interesting."

"At last we get to hear the defense," Anne said. "Glen Raw-lins, the reporter on the case, told me Mr. Nesting has received death threats. It's the biggest story of the year."

"We have the trial at 10 a.m. and the game at 7 p.m. I'll pick you up for the game at 6:30.

"I'll be ready," Anne said.

"I like the music," Jack said, "especially 'Midnight at the Oa-sis.' Would you like to dance?"

"Yes."

Jack felt Anne's body swaying up against his. They circled slowly around the room. The formal dance holds faded when Anne's arms wrapped around Jack's waist and Jack's arms around Anne's shoulders. They hugged close and kissed often. In between songs they sipped their wine. Soon they were on the couch, kissing and caressing.

"Let's go up to my veranda," Anne said.

Jack picked up the bottle of wine and the glasses, following Anne to her bedroom. From there they walked out onto the veranda, leaving the glass door open. Jack put the bottle and glasses down on a small round table. They sat on a small cushioned love seat. Jack poured some more wine. At first they looked out at the city lights and Greenville's Jefferson Butte silhouetted in the distance. Jack's arm slipped around Anne. They sipped merlot and hugged. From the living room the music filtered up the stairs. Soon they were dancing again to the slow music. The moon was coming up in the east. Jack carefully picked Anne up in his arms and carried her inside. In the bedroom he gently set her down. Clothes dropped to the floor. Then they eased their way under the covers.

Chapter 43

The court case of Emerald County vs. George Brown convened Tuesday morning. The previous day, the prosecution's evidence had accused George Brown of arson and murder in Nahato.

George Brown, the defendant, sat with his attorney, Virgil Nesting, at a table in the front of the courtroom. Jack wondered how Virgil would handle the defense. If it had been a baseball game he knew Virgil was down five to nothing. Virgil needed a home run. Jack felt that the only way Virgil could save his client would be if someone confessed to the crime, and that wasn't likely.

Jack, Anne, and Freddie sat in the crammed citizens' section. Anne nudged Jack.

"George looks better today."

"He's finally getting his side of the story told," Jack said.

"It's about time," Freddie whispered.

The fifty or so people in the courtroom all seemed to be talking at once when the bailiff ordered quiet in the courtroom.

"Is the defense ready?" Judge Anthony Belton asked.

"Yes, your Honor," Virgil Nesting said in a commanding voice. Virgil was dressed in a loose-fitting gray suit and his trademark red tie. His tall, lean frame advanced to the jury box. His ponytail swung from side to side as he looked into the eyes of the jurors.

"Ladies and gentlemen of the jury, today you will hear George's defense. The prosecution's case is just too perfect, and I personally detect a frame-up. I will show that George is an innocent man. All this stuff that the prosecution is telling you about George wanting revenge is balderdash. Sure, George was mad. Wouldn't you be mad if you just had the daylights knocked out of you? He was beaten up because of the color of his skin. Were Mr. Larry Bales and his customers prejudiced against Negroes? The sign over the tavern's doorway would certainly indicate that. Together they committed a violent crime attacking the defendant. So, does intolerance play a part in this trial? I contend that it does. The defendant is on trial for his life because he is a black man."

"Yes, yes!" Jack heard Freddie utter. "Let's get the truth out!"

"Did George really take twenty-five gallons of gas? Was George in any kind of condition to run around the mill throwing gas on rags? Ladies and gentlemen, he had just been beaten up. He had two severely cracked ribs. Have you ever had a cracked rib? If you had, you'd know that it's very hard to move without intense pain. All George wanted was *five* gallons of gas. I contend that is all he took. Oh yes, he probably splashed another gallon on the ground in his hurry to get out of there. So, yes he's guilty of stealing maybe six gallons. There's evidence around the pump that a lot more gas was spilled and I think the perpetrator of the arson was also in a hurry.

"The tavern's proprietor refused to let George use the tavern's phone. George wanted to call his wife. He wanted to tell her to bring some gas to Nahato so he could drive home. Bales told George the phone was out of order. That's when George asked for help from the patrons. No one volunteered. In fact, instead of helping George, they almost killed him.

"When George regained consciousness after the beating, he got up and went directly to his car for the gas can. He needed gas in order to drive home.

"The prosecution says that George cannot account for where he was when the fire was started. They say he doesn't have an alibi. The prosecution is dead wrong. After George got the gas, he emptied it into his gas tank. Then George tried to drive home.

Halfway there George parked his car along the side of the road and fell into a coma. Did he have an alibi? Ladies and gentlemen, I contend that George is lucky to be alive. When he woke up, he drove home. It's true no one saw him, but George's condition explains his whereabouts.

"I intend to prove here that George was beaten because of his skin color, and that George's injuries were so severe he could not possibly have set the fire that burned down the Nahato lumber mill and tavern."

"That's just what I've been saying," Freddie whispered.

Jack nodded his head in agreement.

"My first witness is Larry Bales, proprietor of the Nahato Tavern."

Mr. Bales came forward, was sworn in, and took the witness stand.

"What a vile man," Anne said.

"Mr. Bales, how long has that 'No Niggers' sign been above your tavern's door?"

"About four years."

"Why was it there?"

"I and a few customers decided we wanted to keep my place primarily for white folk. Like a club. Some clubs prohibit women don't they?"

"Yes," Virgil said. "Would you have allowed me into your establishment? I'm part Nez Perce and my skin is dark."

"I have nothing against Indians."

"What do you have against black people?"

"Way to go, give it to him, bravo!" Freddie said softly.

"Listen," Mr. Bales said. "I wanted to keep my place for the local white population. We built our community. Negroes aren't a part of it. Is that so hard to understand?"

"It's very hard to understand. First of all your tavern is not a private club. It's a tavern open to the public. Is not George a member of the public?"

"My sign clearly warns niggers there might be a big risk should they come in. I think any Negro would heed that warning. That's why I put the sign up there."

"Yet George was not coming in as a customer. George needed help, that's all, help. He needed to call his wife so she could bring him some gas. You told George your phone was out of order. I've checked with the phone company and they say your phone was working. Why didn't you let George use your phone?"

"Because he wasn't supposed to be in my place! To put it bluntly, I wanted George to leave."

"Please correct me if I'm wrong. The way I understand it is that George was backing out of your place when he was tripped. Then you asked your customers if anyone wanted to fight George?"

"I wanted George to leave. My customers didn't want George in my place either. They took it on themselves to enforce my rules. We took George outside. Dave Summers and George fought. George lost. We made sure he was alive and moved him to a safe place in my parking lot."

"How many customers were in the tavern that evening?"

"About twenty."

"Did your customers see George carrying a gas can?"

"Yes."

"Did they see him carrying rags?"

"No."

"Your sign would indicate, sir, that you are a racist. Is that true?"

"It's the white people who built our country. I would like Negroes to accept their place in our society. If that type of reasoning is racist, then I'm a racist."

"Did you call for an ambulance?"

"We never call for ambulances when there are fights in my

place. We don't feel it's necessary to get the police involved in simple fights. George was still alive. These types of fights happen all the time."

"Did anyone else call for an ambulance to help George?"

"No."

"If George had died, would you have cared?"

"No."

Jack heard Anne's gasp and saw her hand move to cover her mouth. A lot of other people gasped too, causing the bailiff to order "Quiet in the courtroom."

"That's all, Mr. Bales," Virgil said.

Jack heard Freddie whisper, "Way to go, Virgil. Way to go!"

"My next witness is Dr. Ferguson."

Virgil followed the doctor as he was sworn in, and then the doctor took the witness stand. He was a white man in his mid forties with rosy checks.

"Dr. Ferguson, how long has the defendant been a patient of yours?"

"Roughly ten years."

"In your opinion is George a vindictive man?"

"No."

"Does George hate Caucasians?"

"If he does, he's never mentioned it to me."

"How badly was George injured?"

"He'd lost three front teeth and had two cracked ribs."

"Would his wounds have allowed him to throw twenty-five gallons of gas on the Nahato mill?"

"George was in a lot of pain. Yet men do miraculous feats under similar duress. I can't really make a judgment like that."

"Would it be highly unlikely that he set the fire?"

"Yes."

"Is it possible that he fell into a coma when he stopped his car to take a rest while trying to drive home?"

"Very possible."

"When you treated George's wounds, did you notice any type of wood smoke on his clothes?"

"Only cigarette smoke."

"In your opinion, is the defendant the type of person that would burn down a lumber mill and tavern?"

"No."

"No more questions. You may step down. My next witness is fire chief Wilbur Caulkins."

Jack felt Anne's hand clutch his. He saw a smile of approval on her face.

"Great defense," Anne whispered.

Jack felt a breeze as the chief walked by him to take the oath.

"Sir," Virgil asked, "Did your department do a thorough search of George's criminal record?"

"Yes."

"Does he have a criminal record?"

"I found only one disorderly conduct citation. He fulfilled the requests of the court at that time."

"Is there any record of George setting fires?"

"No."

"Is it possible that the fire could have been set by a person obsessed with fire, a pyromaniac?"

"Highly unlikely. It is yet to be determined if pyromaniacs even exist. Most fires are set to get revenge, children's play, accidents, to cover up a murder, to destroy evidence, to collect insurance, and so on. There's usually a reason a fire is set. If a pyromaniac existed he'd be a monster. Evidence shows this to be highly improbable."

178

"Then you think this fire was a deliberate act of arson?"

"Yes."

"That's all. You may step down. Would Mr. Hugh Lofton, owner of the Nahato lumber mill, please come forward and be sworn in?"

"Mr. Lofton, did Sam Taylor have any enemies?"

"None. He'd been employed with the mill for over twenty years. Everyone liked Sam."

"Did Sam smoke cigarettes?"

"Yes. But Sam was a cautious man."

"Did he drink on the job?"

"I suppose so, although we don't allow alcohol on the premises. He could have taken a few nips."

"Was he unstable, or had he any mental problems that you were aware of?"

"He had his bouts with depression. But he lived with it and still did his job. Sir, he had nothing to do with this fire."

"Did your business have anything to gain from the fire?"

"Your honor, I resent this question!"

"Answer the question to the best of your ability," the judge responded.

"Well, I'll get my building and equipment replaced. But over all I come out the loser. The fire disrupted business, left a lot of destruction, and led to the loss of a dear friend."

"That's all, Mr. Lofton. At this time I'd like to ask my next witness, Mrs. Sam Taylor, if she would come forward please." She was a middle aged woman with a fragile frame and stark white hair. She was sworn in, and then took the witness stand.

"Mrs. Taylor would you consider your husband to be a stable, sane man?"

"On occasions Sam would get severely depressed. At those times he drank heavily. He wasn't a mean man, but when he

179

drank like that he was hard on himself."

"What exactly do you mean, 'hard on himself?'"

"He'd lock himself in our bedroom, with the blinds pulled and lights out. Then he'd listen to loud music, like he was trying to block out his thoughts. You could hear music all over the house. At times his face showed a lot of anguish—lips snarled and mean eyes. He would carry on like that for days, and then he'd pop out of it and become his regular self again."

"Had he ever contemplated suicide?"

"Yes."

"Could he have started the fire in an attempt to kill himself?"

"Possibly."

"That's all, you may step down. That ends my defense for today, your Honor."

"This court will reconvene at 10 a.m. on Thursday morning," Judge Belton ordered.

When Virgil pushed through the courtroom doors he was greeted with a mob of people. Reporter Glen Rawlings tried to ask some questions but was brushed off, with a "No comment." Jack, Anne, and Freddie waited in the hallway, hoping to talk with the defense attorney. When Virgil stepped out of the mob, Jack called out.

"Over here!" Jack waved.

"Let's go into a counseling room," Virgil said.

When the door closed behind Jack the noisy throng was silenced. They all took seats around the table.

"What are your feelings about the case?" Freddie said.

"Not good," Virgil said. "Did you notice the jurors? I don't think they were buying my reasonable doubts. I need something big to finish this trial, some new bit of evidence. I have one more

180

day to prepare. I wish I could be more optimistic."

"Weren't you going to ask Dave Summers questions?" Jack said.

"I've decided to wait until Thursday to question him. I think it will have more impact at the conclusion of the trial. What about tonight's game? Can we beat the Ravens?"

"Dave will be playing," Jack said. "Macomb is pitching, and Freddie will be playing center field as usual."

"I need to bust out of my slump," Freddie said. "If Dave and I can start hitting again there's no way they can win. We've got to help Richard."

"Good luck this evening," Virgil said. "Our futures are in the hands of destiny. Anything can happen."

Chapter 44

As usual, Jack and Anne sat in the reserved seating section behind home plate. It was Tuesday evening and the second game in the pennant series was about to be played. The outfield grass had been carefully mowed. The big light standards popped on, and as the sun settled in the west, shade settled over the fans, seven thousand of them. The national anthem had been sung and the Giants were warming up on the field.

"Dave's playing first base," Anne said.

"Yes, Rudy will have to sit this one out," Jack said. "We're hoping Dave can lead us to a victory. Grover Marino is scheduled to pitch."

"But I thought Richard..."

"He broke team rules last night, and didn't get to bed until 2 in the morning. Burt was really pissed. He cussed him out, and told him Marino was starting. That's Richard in the bull pen working out.

I've asked Virgil Nesting to sit with us tonight. He said he would."

"Oh, good," Anne said.

"I think he's going to get George off."

"I'm not so sure," Anne said. "He didn't seem that hopeful this morning. I'm glad George was able to retain him, though. At least he's got a fighting chance."

"Play ball!" the umpire said.

"We've got to win tonight," Jack said.

In the top of the first inning Grover couldn't control his pitches. They were high, in the dirt, and way outside. Burt made many trips to the mound to consult with him. Nothing would calm Grover. After walking three batters the fourth was hit in the shoulder.

"Ouch!" Anne said. "That must smart."

"And it forced a run across the plate," Jack said. "We need to get Grover off the mound." Then Jack saw Burt motioning for Richard Macomb to come in. "Good."

"I know you can do it Richard," Anne whispered. Richard struck out two batters and the third hit a fly ball to center field. Freddie Toll sprinted after the ball. He made a fantastic leap, flying horizontally to snag the ball. He landed crashing on his right shoulder. The fans cheered.

"Great catch!" Anne said.

The crowd roared as the Giants came to bat trailing one to nothing.

"Do the Giants have a chance?" Virgil said as he took his seat next to Jack.

"Hey good to see you, glad you could make it," Jack said. "I think if Richard can make it through the game without getting injured we have a chance." The Ravens began warming up on the field, pitching and in-fielding balls. "Have you come up with any more ideas about getting George off?"

"I need more information," Virgil said. "When I return to my office tonight, I'm supposed to have investigative reports on my desk."

"Who are you investigating?"

"Larry Bales, some of his customers, and Dave Summers."

"Why Dave?" Jack said.

"He was involved in that fight. I want more background information. I need it before I put him on the stand."

184

"I checked his criminal record," Anne said leaning over Jack's knees. "I couldn't find a thing on him."

"I'm hoping to find something, maybe a pattern of behavior, anything," Virgil said. "I have a strange feeling about him."

"Pitching for the Ravens is, Walt Thurmond," the announcer said.

The umpire dusted home plate, "Play ball."

"Here we go," Jack said. Freddie Toll stood in the batter's box, slowly swinging his bat, concentrating on the Ravens' pitcher. "I'm hoping Freddie can pull out of his slump." The count went to three balls and two strikes. Freddie kept fouling.

"Come on, Freddie," Anne shouted. "Yes! Freddie got a hit!" she cried. Freddie ran to first base as his single fell into right field. He threatened to take second but the right fielder got the ball there first. Freddie returned to first base.

Jack saw his smile of relief.

"Oh, good, his slump's over." Anne said.

"I've heard that in division playoffs," Virgil said, "The team that wins the first game usually wins the series."

"That's true," Jack said. "But don't tell anyone else, OK?"

"Mum's the word." Virgil said, placing his big hand over his mouth.

"Gifford is at bat," Anne said.

"Strike one," said the umpire as he shot up a hand.

"You son of a bitch, that was a ball!" a loud heavy-set fan roared from behind Jack and Anne. Jack cringed at the outburst.

"Strike two!"

"You asshole, put on some glasses!"

"Many people were staring at the loudmouth. A few more obnoxious words brought security.

One guard grabbed the man's arm and attempted to move him off. The man jerked his arm away.

"Call for police backup."

"I'm going! You don't have to call for the police," the drunken man replied. He stood and staggered off towards the exits, with two guards right behind him.

"Thank goodness," Anne said. "I hate people like that." The last pitch went by Gifford so fast he didn't have time to react. "Strike three! Oh no! Gifford's out." The next batter was Ron Stewart, second baseman. On the third pitch he hit a grounder between the pitcher's legs. It hopped over the second base bag into center field. Freddie ran to second, and Ron was safe on first base. Dave Summers came to bat. The crowd hooted, knowing that Dave had the wallop to drive in runs. Dave took a big swing and shot one over the left field fence ending his slump. Three runs crossed home plate. The Giants leapt into the lead. The crowd roared.

The Ravens made two more outs and the first inning ended. The score remained 3 to 1 through the top of the ninth inning, when the Ravens threatened to score. With one out, Don Wellington hit a single to left field. Duane Wilson fielded the ball, throwing to Stewart at second base. Then Bud Cordon hit a double off the right field fence. Sam Collins fielded the ball by throwing to Dave on first. Runners were on second and third when Pete Gussy came to bat. He hit a ball that skipped towards Gifford at third. Gifford picked up the ball, tagged Don Wellington who was off the base, then threw a sizzler to Dave on first. The ball beat Gussy by a millisecond. "You're out," said the first base umpire.

Bob Zorr, Raven's manager, raced to first base. He was nose to nose with the umpire. Jack could hear Zorr's loud accusations, "Check with the other umpire! I saw that clearly and Gussy beat the ball. It was close but he was SAFE!" Zorr left the field, walking backwards, hands gesturing wildly, and then he threw his hat on the ground. "He was safe, I tell you!"

All in vain, Jack thought. No matter what Zorr could have done, the simple truth was that the Giants had won the second game. The crowd roared and raced onto the field. The Giants

186

headed for the dressing room. The Ravens' Thurmond had held the Giants to no runs after that first disastrous inning. Richard Macomb had struck out seven batters and allowed only four hits. Richard was the hero of the game.

"One more game," Jack said.

"I'm looking forward to it," Virgil said. "I'll see you tomorrow night." He left Jack and Anne in their seats, waiting for the crowds to dwindle.

"Did you see the furrows in Virgil's brow," Anne said.

"Yes, he's worried. I wouldn't be surprised if he worked all night on the case. He only has one more day to prepare. These games are a good outlet for him. I'm glad he's coming tomorrow night."

"Me too," Anne said. "Jack, we may win the pennant!"

Chapter 45

Later that night there was a light in the mayor's office window. The shades were drawn. Two shadows crept about, and then they settled. Tom Brand swayed back in his creaking chair, his toes barely touching the floor. Suddenly the mayor's chair squealed upright. Ridley's head snapped towards the mayor.

"Yes?" Ridley asked.

"Damn," Tom said. "We have a financial bonanza for this city and the stupid game of baseball is undermining it. We've got banks and businesses interested in the stadium property. Millions can be made. Millions of tax dollars could be raised. It's ridiculous! What's wrong with this city anyway? What happened to Marge? We need her, and her husband's money. That backstabbing slut says she's not with us anymore. She won't give us the money for a political campaign to remove Jack on the council. Well, damn her. We'll do this thing without her. It just means more money for us."

"Amen," Ridley said.

"We've got to be ready at the next council meeting. We'll have Jack recuse himself because of his personal interest in the stadium. That will leave two votes for us and three against. Are any of the other councilmen waffling?"

"George Putman could be," Ridley said.

"Let's ask George to join us. We've got to be careful, though. We don't want to spill the beans until we're sure he's our man. George is no fool. He knows a good opportunity. Let's make him a big offer before next week's council meeting. OK?"

"Yes, absolutely. We have no other options," Ridley said.

Chapter 46

At last it was the night of the big deciding game. The players in the Giants' dressing room were preparing to go to the field. They needed to win. Burt shook his head. He had never thought this game possible. He knew that the players responsible for it were Dave Summers, Richard Macomb, and Freddie Toll. Their coming to play for the Greenville Giants had been a stroke of luck. Burt knew that tonight's game would be a thriller. Big league scouts had already checked in with him. It was his job to prepare this team for tonight's battle.

Burt looked around the dressing room. He saw men in various stages of dress. Some fully suited, others tying shoes or buttoning shirts. He needed to jack them up and build their confidence.

"Listen up, everyone. I want to say a few words before we go out onto the field. I'm starting Dave Summers as pitcher tonight. The rest of the line-up is posted on the door. You guys are about to play one of the most important games of your career. If you win, you'll make history here in Greenville. Your achievement will be unprecedented. You'll be able to look back on this championship game as one of your fondest memories. You've been outstanding this baseball season. So don't get nervous now, just think of it as another league game and play the best you can."

Duane Wilson waved his hand frantically.

"What is it Duane?"

"Sorry to interrupt, coach, but I've got something important to say."

"Then say it."

Duane moved a chair into the center of the room. He stepped up on it, his rabbit foot dangling from his belt. "I don't normally talk well in front of people. But I've got to say this. Guys, this is my last season. There's no chance I'll be going to the majors. I'm too old. Anyway, I've been there before. But I want you all to know something—this has been the best fucking season of my life. I want us to go out there and win this game. We've done it the whole season. We can do it now. Your futures may be riding on how well you perform tonight, so do your fucking best! I'm finished, coach."

"Thank you, Duane. Go get 'em guys, make me proud!"

Chapter 47

Jack and Anne were in line waiting to go into the stadium. Thousands of people mingled restlessly for the gates to open.

"They're opening the gates," Jack said. The crowd poured through the turnstiles filling the stadium's concourse. Some rushed inside the stadium to get the best general admission seats.

Jack and Anne climbed the stadium's stairs to the heart of the covered seating section. Fans were grabbing seats and setting up residency. Jack and Anne held hands as they stepped down to their reserved seats behind home plate. It was a beautifully clear evening. On the field, linesmen were finishing marking boundaries. Two umpires stood ready. The moon glowed in the east hills, larger then Jack had ever seen it before. Huge reddish clouds hovered around it. Could I ask for anything better? Jack thought. A moon-filled sky, preparations for the biggest baseball game of the year, thousands of people around. It's my opportunity and I'm not going to miss it. As the Giants were warming up on the field and the Ravens busy swinging bats, Jack turned to Anne.

"Anne," Jack said, and she turned her attention to him with a smile. That lovely smile almost made him lose his nerve. "I've never said this before and believe me it's hard for me to say."

"What?"

"I've never enjoyed the company of anyone as much as I've enjoyed sharing moments with you. These past few months have been the most wonderful of my life. I'm hopelessly in love with you."

"I feel the same way about you," Anne said.

Jack took Anne's hands in his. His looked into her blue eyes. "Anne, will you marry me?"

Anne looked to the field. Tears flooded her eyes. "What a special thing to ask," and then looking back into his eyes, "Of course I will." They kissed.

Just then Virgil arrived and took his seat. "Am I interrupting something?"

"Yes—the most important event in my life," Jack said. "I just asked Anne to marry me and she accepted. We're engaged to be married."

"My congratulations!" Virgil said. "A wonderful moment indeed!" He shook Jack's hand. Then he bent over Jack and kissed Anne. "Jack, you chose a grand place to pop the question. I love you both and it's great that you two have decided to get hitched. Wow, I didn't expect to be a part of so much emotion. Now we just have to throw that emotion out there to the Giants so they can win this game."

"Pitching for the Ravens is Patrick Merick," the announcer said.

"Uh-oh," Anne said. "They have that ex-Yankee pitching for them. They're putting up their best."

"Pitching for the Giants is Dave Summers." The latter was greeted by an explosion of cheers.

"Dave's no pushover, although he hasn't done that well lately," Jack said. "Burt must have decided to put him in at the last minute. Big surprise!"

The umpire dusted off home plate and pulled his mask down. "Play ball!"

Dave didn't waste much time—Bud Cordon, Pete Gussy, and Joe Knowles went hitless. Merick showed why he had pitched for the Yankees. His slider, curve, and knuckleball outfoxed Fred, Gifford, and Stewart. They went down like tipped dominoes. By the top of the fifth inning the game was scoreless. Jack and Virgil shelled peanuts and drank beer while Anne ate a hamburger.

Hank Cunningham, the Ravens' center fielder, stepped into the batter's box. Dave's pitch was a fastball. Cunningham smacked it, and had the first single in the game. It landed in right field where Sam Collins fielded it by throwing to second baseman Stewart. Cunningham rested at first base. That brought Yankee pitcher Merick to the plate.

"One pitcher trying to outsmart the other," Jack said. "I wonder who will win." The first pitch hissed its way low and outside towards Merick.

Merick reached for it, striking the ball into right field for a single. Outfielder Collins threw the ball to shortstop Ben Martin. With Cunningham on second and Merick on first the left-handed slugging sensation Ted Peck came to bat. This series of pitches was a real duel between Dave and Ted. At the same time Dave had to keep an alert eye on the runners, throwing to the second baseman three times. With the count full, three balls and two strikes, Peck fouled four consecutive pitches. In desperation, Dave tried a curve that was low and inside. Peck belted it out of the park. Three runs crossed the plate. Burt ran out to the mound. Burt told Dave to replace Rudy at first, and then motioned for Macomb, who was warming up in the bull pen, to come out to the mound. While Macomb warmed up, Jack looked over to Virgil.

"Macomb pitched last night. No use trying to second guess Burt, I hope he knows what he's doing."

"I think the lad can do it. Listen!" Virgil pointed to the field, were Macomb was throwing fastballs. "Burt's glove is cracking like thunder claps."

"That kid has power," Jack said. "Virgil, has your investigation uncovered anything about Dave?"

"Actually, it has." Virgil spoke low so only Jack could hear. "I've found a chain of fires that follows Dave around the country. The first and maybe the most hellacious was the fire that killed his mother and father. Dave was fifteen when that happened. With the insurance money he's roamed around the country ever since, playing bush-league baseball and volunteering as a firefighter. In some of the fires he was a hero—like the Junction City fire, and a fire in Los Angeles where he saved a child of four. Yet people have also died in these fires, just like the Nahato fire where Sam Taylor met his death. I want to find out what's his attraction to fire."

"Hey, Canfield is coming to bat," Anne said. Macomb's first pitch was a strike.

No doubt about it, Jack thought, Macomb was in rhythm. He could almost hear Macomb's famous buzz-ball whoosh towards home plate. He didn't appear tired. Three batters came and went. Unfortunately, Merick did the same in the bottom of the fifth. Both repeated in the sixth, retiring the batters. Soon it was the bottom of the seventh and the Giants still trailed three to zero. Fans stood for the customary singing of "Take Me Out to the Ball Game." When the song finished a trumpet tooted. That's when Jack, Anne, and Virgil raised their arms skyward and yelled "charge."

"I don't know much about Dave," Jack said. "But I find it hard to believe he'd set fires just to set fires. You might be harming your case by that line of reasoning. I think he'd say 'I fight fires to put them out, I don't set them.'"

"I tend to agree with you," Virgil said. "But there's a disturbing pattern here. If he's the cause of these fires then we have a demon on our hands—a pyromaniac. I know what the fire chief said, that it's highly improbable. I don't care if it turns out I look like a bumbling ass, after examining the investigative reports, it's my opinion that Dave set the Nahato fire."

"That's a wild accusation," Jack said. "I hope you'll be ready to prove it. Hey, Dave's coming to bat." On the third pitch Dave belted the ball from the park. Freddie Toll, who'd been warming up in the batter's circle, was up next. On the second pitch he also hit a home run. Stewart singled. Gifford hit a double that brought in Stewart. The game was now tied at three to three. Bob Zorr rushed to the pitcher's mound. Thurmond was summoned from the dugout, and Merick walked from the field. When he reached the dugout, he threw his mitt against the bench. Jack saw his angry face. Thurmond retired the side.

The eighth inning went scoreless. The top of the ninth brought the Ravens to bat. Pete Gussy singled to center field. Freddie fielded and threw to Stewart on second base. On the next pitch Gussy ran for second, hoping for a steal. But Burt caught the pitched ball and in one easy motion threw a scorcher to second base. Stewart caught the ball and brought his glove down to touch Gussy, whose spikes were in the air. As he slid into second, Gussy's spikes ripped through Stewart's calf, causing him to drop the ball.

"Safe!" the umpire said.

Blood stained Stewart's pants. He limped from the field. Burt motioned Dave to replace him, and pointed to Rudy in the dugout. Rudy went to cover first base. Macomb then walked Knowles. Two men were on base when the powerful hitter, Ted Peck, advanced to the plate. The assemblage of Portland fans cheered vigorously.

"My God," Jack said.

"This is awful," Anne said.

"Looks grim," Virgil said.

Another pitching duel ensued. There were so many foul balls Jack thought the game would go on all night. He knew Richard was throwing everything he had, including his famous buzz-ball. Finally, Ted hit a howitzer blast straight at Macomb. He hit the dirt. The ball started to gain altitude; the base runners were so sure of a hit that they took off for third and second base. Dave made a spectacular kangaroo leap, stretching his gloved hand in the air.

The ball smashed into his mitt, whack! "Ugh" echoed across the diamond and into the stadium. He came down just in time to tag second base. Then he chased down and tagged Knowles who was trying to run back to first base. Three outs. The side was retired. Everyone, including Virgil, stood in the stands and applauded Dave's remarkable play.

"Unbelievable, rarely happens!" Jack heard Virgil mutter. The Giants ran for the dugout. The Ravens took the field for the bottom of the ninth. "This game could go on all night if no one scores." Sam Collins was up first. He hit a grounder to Pete Gussy at short stop. It was an easy throw to first.

"One out," Anne said. That brought Rudy to the plate. He hit a grounder to first base, where he was called out. Freddie advanced to the plate. "Come on, Freddie," Anne clapped, sitting on the edge of her seat.

The first pitch was a fastball. It zoomed over the plate. Freddie watched it calmly.

"Strike one!" uttered the umpire. A few hecklers hooted from the stands.

Thurmond's arm flew up for the next pitch. The arm came down, catapulting the ball towards home plate. Freddie had anticipated another fastball so he was ready when the ball scorched towards him. His hit took off like a cannon blast and hit against the center field fence with a thud. Cunningham bobbled the ball. Freddie was running like the wind. The first base coach yelled, "Keep going!" Freddie flew to second at a gallop. The third base coach motioned to keep running. The ball was in the air from center field to third. Freddie slid into the base and collided with Ted Peck. The ball popped out of his mitt and rolled towards the stands. "Don't run! Stay on base," the third base coach told Freddie. Fred bounced to his feet, watching Peck scramble after the ball. Ignoring the coach's call, Freddie took off for home plate. When Peck got the ball he threw for the catcher. The ball and runner arrived together. The umpire was on his hands and knees watching as Freddie dove headfirst for the plate, Freddie barely squirmed around the catcher's outstretched arms.

198

"Safe!" the umpire roared. The crowd went nuts—absolutely nuts. The team of rejects had accomplished the impossible. They had just won the Pacific North League pennant! Fans flooded the field, congratulating players. Macomb, Freddie, and Dave were carried around the infield on players' shoulders. The players uncorked champagne bottles. Mini geysers erupted all over the infield. Newspaper photographers angled for their best shots, and bulbs flashed. Fans shared in the celebration by drinking with the players. Jack and Anne hurried to the field.

Burt was congratulating the players. He shook hands and pounded backs. His smile told all of his players how proud he was at their performance.

"Freddie, you played crazy. You were told not to run home, yet you risked it anyway. I'm proud of you for making that decision. I think pennants are won because someone makes a gutsy move, one that's not expected. Anyway, my hat's off to you. You won the game for us. Congratulations."

"And you Macomb, what a performance! Sorry I threw you in there on short notice, but damn it, I knew you could do it. Stay healthy and I'll make sure the major league scouts hear about you!" Burt wanted to congratulate Dave. He saw him standing off to the side. People were congratulating him, yet he seemed preoccupied. Oh sure, he was smiling and taking all the back slaps in a jovial way. Yet Burt thought he looked antsy, anxious to leave. He walked over to Dave with his hand outstretched. Dave grabbed it. "Great game, Dave! How does it feel to be a champion?"

"Great, really great!"

"Are you going to play for us next year? We could win another pennant if you play." Dave's happy demeanor changed sharply.

"No sir, I won't be back. I've been recruited to play for a triple A minor league team in El Paso, Texas. I'll be leaving town as soon as the trial is over. As you probably know, Virgil Nesting has subpoenaed me as a witness in the George Brown case."

"I'd hate to have to face Nesting," Burt said. "He's a cagey attorney. Be careful. I'm sorry to hear that you've decided to leave. You're a great player. That play you made in the top of the ninth, putting out three players was phenomenal. Outside of that slump you were in, you played outstanding ball. Hey man, no hard feelings, I wish you all the best." Burt shook Dave's hand again and moved off into the crowd. His champagne glass was refilled and he toasted his players again for the umpteenth time.

Jack had noticed a grim Virgil leave the stands when the game ended. He knew Virgil would have to confront a man who was one of Greenville's most popular citizens, and to call Dave a pyromaniac? No way. Virgil was gambling he could get George off by creating doubt in jurors' minds. But by taking this approach he might be risking George's freedom. Jack didn't think it would work. He didn't think much of Dave personally, but he admired his baseball athleticism. Jack and Anne kept their distance from Dave, chatting mostly with Burt and Freddie. Burt had casually mentioned that Dave would be leaving the team, going to Texas. Jack was relieved to hear it. He thought Dave a great athlete, but he brought divisiveness to the team with his racial views. Jack thought there would be more black players playing for the Giants in the future. Soon the evening's excitement ebbed. Players began leaving the field, so Jack and Anne headed for his station wagon.

Chapter 48

Once inside Anne's cozy apartment, Jack and Anne headed for the veranda with a bottle of merlot. The cork popped. They settled down on Anne's love seat, looking up at the stars and the outline of Jefferson Butte in the distance. Jack poured the wine.

"Did you ever think all this would happen?" Anne asked. "Because of you, Greenville was able to win a pennant, the most important baseball achievement here in years. You must be very proud."

"I am," Jack said. "Proud of Burt, proud of the team, and proud of you. We overcame a lot of roadblocks. If only my parents could have seen this championship game."

"Maybe they did," Anne said.

"Well, if they did," Jack said, "they're probably all abuzz about my proposal of marriage to you."

"They're probably saying, Jack's gone nuts. He's asked a woman sportswriter to be his wife. Women don't write about sports. They're supposed to teach school and become nurses."

"Wait just a minute," Jack said, "If those ancestors have any qualms, they'd better talk to me or get out! They're just jealous. I'm going to have the most nervy, daring, and beautiful wife of anyone in our family."

"And to think it was Greenville's stadium that brought us together," Anne said.

Suddenly Jack sat upright.

"What is it?" Anne said.

"Something that Virgil said during the game. He thinks Dave is a pyromaniac!"

"That's silly," Anne said.

"That's exactly what I thought, too," Jack said.

"He's a hero when ever there's a fire," Anne said. "What about Mr. Bartel? Dave saved his life. Remember how he pulled him from that grocery store fire in Junction City? Dave risked his life."

"That's true. Still, he's always around terrible fires," Jack said. "Virgil told me Dave's parents died in a huge fire when Dave was fifteen years old."

"Maybe that's why he fights fires," Anne said. "To make up for not saving them."

"You could be right," Jack said.

"Yet, if he did kill his parents," Anne said, "That means he burned down his home and the people dearest to him."

"My God, if he'd kill his own parents he'd destroy anything," Jack said. "You know, I found him at the stadium last week."

"I remember you telling me," Anne said. "He pushed you and wouldn't explain why he was there. Is it possible he was preparing the stadium for a fire?"

"Damn!" Jack said. "How could we be so blind? We'd better get over there."

Chapter 49

Jack parked his station wagon in the Greenville Stadium parking lot. On their way to the stadium they'd seen Dave's yellow Cadillac on 19th Street, a couple of blocks away.

"Let's go check under the south part of the stadium," Jack said. "I want to make sure nothing's been tampered with." They walked up to the gate in the cyclone fence.

"That's strange," Jack said. "There's usually a lock on this gate. It's gone." The gate swung open with a creak. The parking lot lights receded behind them as they walked towards the concourse to the south side of the stadium. Light from lampposts on a nearby street trickled through trees. They stepped over concession trash along the deserted concourse. Vendors' empty counters gaped at them. Barely visible signs advertised popcorn, bagels, peanuts, and beer. Finally they reached the door that would take them under the stadium. The door was open. Jack could hear someone moving around inside.

"You stay here," Jack whispered. "I'm going in." Jack eased silently into the cavern. Once inside he waited while his eyes adjusted to the low light. Finally he could make out the massive wooden beams that shot upwards and pierced the underside of the stadium. Jack moved from one beam to the next toward the noise. Then he smelled gas. He heard the sloshing of liquid on walls and beams. He saw the shadow of a man moving around the perimeter spilling out the gas. He heard Anne trip on something.

"Who's there?" A voice called out of the gloom—Dave

Summers' voice.

"It's me, Dave," Jack said, stepping out into the open. "Don't do this—we know about you and the fires."

Anne quickly hid behind a beam, out of sight.

"Where are you?" Dave said. "I see you now." Dave walked up to Jack. Jack put up a hand to keep Dave back.

"Keep your distance," Jack said.

Before he could respond Dave unloosed a right fist to Jack's ear. Jack hit the ground, unconscious.

Lying on a six-by-six-foot ledge above the door was Mike Ward. Earlier that evening he'd been chased out of his home by his drunken mother. Mike had sought refuge in the only place he knew that offered him shelter. It wasn't the first time he'd spent the night sleeping on this ledge. He was suddenly awakened by people stirring below. He positioned himself so that his head projected over the edge of his loft. First Dave had entered splashing gas everywhere. Now he saw Jack and Anne come in. Then he saw Dave hit Jack so hard that Jack fell to the ground. Dave found a piece of rope hanging on a nail. He cut a long piece off with his knife and tied Jack to a beam. Jack's head hung limply over his body. Mike heard Anne's attempt to slip out the door.

"Stop!" Dave yelled.

Dave raced after her. Mike heard scuffling outside and a muffled scream. Mike threw his white laundry bag over his shoulder and began climbing down on the connecting studs against the wall. In his rush to get down he slipped and lost his grip on the bag. Out came over 500 baseballs, bouncing and rolling on the south sloping dirt floor. No! He thought. My baseballs! When he got down he quickly hid behind a wooden beam.

Dave dragged Anne back under the stadium. His arm was around her neck, cutting off her supply of air. Her squirming body soon lost consciousness. He stuffed his handkerchief in her mouth and tied her to a beam, not far from Jack.

"Now," Dave said, looking around. "What was that noise I heard in here? Come out," he whispered. "I know some one's in here!" Then louder, "Come out!" He banged his hand on an empty gas can and shouted again. "Come out now!" Suddenly from a catwalk under the seating area, three big raccoons climbed down a beam and sauntered out the door. "Ha!" Dave gave a big sigh of relief. He looked at his two captives, "You won't give me any more trouble. Now to work, building my fire! It may be my best ever!"

Mike was scared to death. He froze behind the beam, thankful for the raccoons that had saved his life. He peered around the beam.

Dave quickly found a full gas can and picked it up in his left hand. In his right hand he flicked Marge's lighter. A circle of light glowed around him. Mike quickly pulled his head back when Dave looked in his direction. When Dave began walking away, Mike peeked out again. The small flame bobbed about and moved towards the south side of the stadium. Suddenly Dave slipped on a baseball and fell with a thud on his back. The can of gas drained out and on him. He tried to get up but whenever he tried to stand he slipped on another baseball. The flame from the lighter ignited his shirt and pants. The harder he tried to stand, the more his clothes caught fire. Then his body began rolling down the slope, as if on a giant conveyor belt of ball bearings, towards the south wall.

Mike heard a loud scream. Then the wall exploded in a burst of flames. Whoosh! Smoke billowed from the area. Mike ran over to Jack.

Jack was recovering, but he was coughing from the smoke. Mike heard Jack tell him to get his pocket knife from his pants pocket. Mike retrieved the knife and cut Jack's ropes. Jack dropped to his knees trying to get his breath.

"Quick," Mike said. "Over here." He pointed to Anne. She

was barely conscious and gagging. Jack staggered over to Anne. He removed the handkerchief from her mouth. Jack took his knife and cut her ropes. Then he picked Anne up in his arms.

"Let's get out of here," Jack said. Mike felt his arm being squeezed and his body pushed from behind and out the door.

"What about Dave?" Mike said.

"He's a goner," Jack said. "That part of the building is already a bonfire. It'd be suicide to go back in there." He carried Anne to the parking lot. Mike trailed behind. Fire trucks began arriving. The building burned ferociously—the biggest, hottest fire Mike had ever seen. Flames soared skyward. The heat was so intense all three of them kept moving back. Anne was coughing, becoming more aware. Jack set her down.

"What happened to Dave?" Anne whispered.

"He slipped on my baseballs," Mike said. "Dave rolled right into the fire. I heard him scream. It was awful."

"That's dreadful," Anne said.

"It was Mike's baseballs that saved our lives," Jack said. "Mike, you're a hero."

"The raccoons saved my life," Mike said. "Dave was demanding that I come out because of the noise he'd heard when I dropped the baseballs. When the raccoons climbed down the beam Dave thought it was them that had caused the noise."

Fire trucks ringed the building, spewing water on the blaze.

"Nothing will save the stadium now," Jack said, lowering his head. "Mike, you come home with me tonight. Tomorrow we'll figure out what's going to happen to you."

"I have an idea," Anne said. "Why don't we adopt Mike?"

Mike looked up, amazed. "Would you? Really?"

"I don't know," Jack said. "Would the courts allow it? Maybe. We've got one of the best attorneys in town. I'm willing to give it a try."

Chapter 50

Only a few charred walls remained of the stadium the next day. The smoldering pit sent whiffs of smoke rising and dissipating in the morning air. Where once a classical stadium had housed the traditional game of baseball, all that remained was blackened rubble.

The bailiff's deep voice called for silence in the court room. Judge Anthony Belton addressed the audience. "Both attorneys have requested a meeting in my office chambers prior to trial summations. I have granted that request."

Jack, Anne, Freddie, and Mike watched from the front row as the men disappeared out a back doorway. George sat alone, his hands still shackled. For the most part the jury sat looking straight ahead. About thirty minutes later the three men returned to the court room. The Judge nodded to the bailiff to order silence.

"It has been brought to the attention of this court that there is extensive evidence connecting Dave Summers with arson-related fires from his hometown of Bainbridge, Alabama, to this last fire, our baseball stadium here in Greenville. Because of the way he planned the fires, Summers had gone undetected. The Nahato fire serves as an example. In this fire, Dave used the town's biased views as a means to divert attention from him. George Brown was the perfect person to blame that fire on. The customers of the tavern blamed George not only because he was at the scene, but also because of the color of his skin. When asked by police, they lied as to where Dave was before the fire. They gave Dave an alibi by saying he was in the tavern. Since then, George's attorney has proven that Dave was not in the tavern. If he was not at the tavern, then where was he? It's clear to this court that he purposely stole rags from George's car. Once doused with gasoline he spread them around the mill and tavern. Then he deliberately ignited them. The inferno caused Sam Taylor's death.

"Fortunately, there are eye witnesses to Dave setting the stadium fire. If not for our witneses, Dave might have escaped detection once again. It's our considered conclusion that Dave had planned this fire for weeks, waiting for the right time to ignite it. He hoped to blame the fire on Marge Beckley by leaving her unique cigarette lighter at the scene of the crime. He'd stolen it from her a few days before the fire.

"According to one witness, Dave's verbal outbursts, while under the stadium, made it evident he was setting the fire for psychological reasons. It's clear to this court that Dave was not setting the fire as an act of revenge. Nor had he hoped to gain a monetary reward, nor was it politically motivated, nor was it a prank. Dave's act was motivated by his own need for a type of delusional gratification.

"Ladies and gentlemen, it is this court's opinion that Dave was a man obsessed with fire. From his childhood days, when it appears he may have purposely set fire to his own house and killed his parents, to his latest fire, he's been using fire to satisfy his own need to watch them. In short, it is this court's reasoned opinion that Dave Summers was a pyromaniac.

"Faced with these statements from the defense, the prosecution has dropped its case against George Brown." The judge smashed his gavel on the table. "George, you are a free man. This case is closed!"

Chapter 51

Jack sat at his customary zone 6 seat to the far left in the council chambers meeting room. The room was hot and stuffy. Jack's forehead perspired slightly from the heat of the overhead lights. The plump Susan Byrd representing zone 5 sat next to him. George Putnam was on her left, then came the mayor, Tom Brand, then came the other representatives. In the audience, Anne and Mike sat near the front row.

"This meeting will now come to order," Mayor Tom Brand said. "The most important issue facing this city is the disposition of the stadium property. We hope to make a decision tonight. This is all we'll discuss, and it's an open meeting. That means the microphone is on. Please come forward and present your ideas. You'll have three minutes each, that's all. Later, councilors will make motions that will provide a path towards dealing with this property. So let's begin."

"My name is Tracie Andrews from zone 2. I'm a seventh grader at Greenville Junior High School. I and my friends all want you to build another stadium. We like going to the games." Then she sang, 'Take Me out to the Ball Game.'

"My name is Sam Bacon, from zone 3. My wish is that if you sell the property you retain a certain part of it so we can build a modern Greenville museum."

"My name is Jason Ridley, from zone 4. I bring good news. I represent wealthy investors who want to buy the property. They propose building medical buildings, an upscale shopping mall, and a high-rise condominium. This would be an excellent use for such a valuable property in the heart of town. Tax dollars will flow and our city will prosper from this development. This is not an idle offer. I'm holding in my hand a check made out to the city of Greenville for $75,000." Ridley waved it in the air. "This is the down payment on the appraised value of the property. If the council accepts the offer tonight, the remainder of the appraised value will be placed in escrow until the close of sale. If you do not accept this offer, there may not be another. You'll be getting the fair market price for the land from reputable investors who want to improve our city. I hope your answer will be yes." Ridley returned to his front row seat with a big smile on his face.

Jack was sad about the stadium, but it was hard for him to visualize a way to resurrect it. All scenarios seemed doomed to failure. The Greenville Giants were history. He had to accept it. Here was a legitimate offer to buy city-owned property. It was a lot of money. The money would help the city. He knew this, but he desperately wanted to stop the sale. Still, the money issue kept coming up in his mind. No one else in Greenville could offer this kind of money. He had to look out for the city's best interests. There was no other alternative. Ridley's offer would have to be grabbed up before the investors left town.

"Since there are no other speakers, we'll bring this part of the meeting to a close," a smiling Tom Brand declared. Then he looked at the councilors. "Is there any discussion?"

Jack felt defeated. He longed to save baseball for Greenville. But what could he do?

"Seeing that there is no discussion, proposals are in order."

"I'd like make a proposal," councilor George Putnam said. "I move we accept Ridley's offer."

"Let's take a vote," the Mayor said.

Suddenly, the big double doors at the back of the meeting room burst open. Marge Beckley came in, followed by a group of men. Heads turned.

"Stop these proceedings. Now!" Marge said, "I have a few words to say to the councilors and people in attendance before any decision is made."

"You're too late, Marge," the mayor said. "The session for citizen input ended three minutes ago. A proposal has been made for the councilors to decide. Now sit down until that vote has been taken."

"I'd better be given time for my presentation," Marge said. "Or I just may implicate a few people in a scandalous attempt at trying to sell our stadium property under less than ethical means."

"All right, all right, the vote will wait until Marge makes her proposal. You have three minutes, and not a second more."

"My proposal may take more than 3 minutes. But I'm sure no one will mind. Right, Mayor?"

"Get on with it," the mayor said.

"When our Greenville Giants won the pennant this year, it suddenly dawned on me how important our team and the game of baseball were to our community. I'll be frank. I didn't like the noise, litter, and cars on University Hill. But you know, that was before I ever went to a baseball game. I've never enjoyed watching anything more then our Greenville Giants winning the pennant. There are a lot of people in the community, and not just children like Tracie, who love to watch the game of baseball. The game allows for our young people to dream of championships, and of playing in the major leagues. The game provides entertainment for our citizens at a reasonable price. Thousands of people are involved and our local commercial industry benefits. Why should we get rid of something so worthwhile to our community?

"As a result, I've contacted the descendants of the lumber barons who supplied the wood for the construction of our stadium back in the 1930s. Lumber companies all over this county contributed. I was hoping they'd donate again. I've also brought with me former baseball players to talk with you about how much the game has meant in their lives. So, I put Frank Youngbold in charge of contacting the lumbermen's descendents. I put Fred Toll in charge of contacting former baseball players. I think we have come up with a plan for making the best use of this property. But first let's hear from Mr. Youngbold."

A man in a three-piece suit stepped up to the microphone. "When Marge presented me with her plan about how she wanted the stadium property used I'll admit I didn't know how to respond. I thought, why stand in the way of progress? We could use the property for the commercial interests that will bring in the most money for our city. Heck, I even wanted to be in on the investment. But as Marge explained to me, there's more then money involved here. She explained that all aspects of our community will benefit—not just the wealthy.

"In the 1930s, my father donated some of the finest Douglas-fir available for the stadium's construction. It put hundreds of people to work—from ditch diggers to architects. Since its construction the stadium has been a recreational center for this town. Why end it? Why not rebuild it? So I presented the idea to my friends—sons and daughters of old lumber company owners. A few of those descendants are with me tonight. This is what we have come up with.

"Last week I visited with Sam Smith, the son of the stadium's original architect. We found his father's old plans for the stadium. The descendents of the lumber companies will provide lumber from tracts of old-growth timber they've set aside. Then we'll finance the rebuilding of the stadium. We've contacted the University of Greenville's architecture department. They've agreed to oversee the project while using it as a teaching model for their students. When finished, the stadium will be one of the finest all-wood stadiums in the country. It will be a destination point for sightseers, and will house our championship baseball team. That's our proposal. Marge has something further to add."

"It gives me a great deal of pleasure to introduce to you Paul Smidly," Marge said. "Paul remembers playing minor league baseball here for the Greenville Giants. He signed many an autograph for the youngsters in this community. He's now in the Baseball Hall of Fame." She handed the microphone to Paul.

"Since I was elected to the Hall of Fame," Paul said, "I've had many honors. But you know, the most important experience in my life was my first professional baseball experience. That happened right here. I'll always remember the fans of this community. They were great. Other players have profited as well. Some of them are with me tonight. They too want to advocate for your new stadium. Fred Toll has something he'd like to add."

"Thank you," Fred said. "Richard Macomb and I look forward to coming here and playing in an exhibition game. We won't be playing here next season because we've signed contracts with major league teams." Cheers and whistles resounded in the room. After the interruption Fred continued, "Here's Marge."

"So this is our proposal: Commercial buildings can be built on the acreage that surrounds the stadium. We're hoping that the combined use of commercial and stadium property will make it profitable for the city. I'm sure the city will profit from the gate receipts at the games, as well as from out-of-town people coming here to watch minor league baseball. Would any member on the council care to formerly propose our proposition?"

Jack's hand shot up. "I propose we rebuild the stadium along the lines suggested, and sell excess acreage to developers."

"We have two proposals before the council," Tom said. "Ridley's will be voted on first. All those in favor raise your hands." George Putman's hand was the only one that rose. "All those in favor of Jack's proposal, raise their hands." It was five to one. Jack's proposal passed. "This meeting is adjourned."

A big smile was on Marge Beckley's face as she and her friends pushed through the big double doors of City Hall. In front of her were Jack, Anne, and Mike. They held hands and nearly skipped down the stairs.

The End

213

About the Author

At San Diego State College, the only class in which Joe Blakely excelled was the writing of history. After graduating with a liberal arts degree, he explored numerous job opportunities, first in real estate sales, then in work as a real estate appraiser. After a number of years in real estate, Joe bought and operated a second hand store. Later, he found a position as a public safety officer for the University of Oregon, from which position he retired in 1999.

Joe Blakely
with wife Saundra Miles

photo by Pauline Rughani

After retirement, Joe returned to his early love of history and began writing about the history of Oregon, supplementing his writings with photographs. His first subject was an old dilapidated building on the bay of Bandon, on the southern Oregon coast. He decided to write about the building's history. To his utter amazement, the editor of the Oregon Historical Quarterly Magazine published "The Nestle Condensary in Bandon" in the winter issue of 2003.

Using that published article as the stage, Joe wrote *The Heirloom*, a novel that takes place on the rugged docks of Bandon in 1921.

"The idea of writing a slice of history followed by a novel appealed to me," Mr. Blakely says. So after writing *Lifting Oregon Out Of The Mud, Building the Oregon Coast Highway*, he wrote his novel *Kidnapped, On Oregon's Coast Highway, 1921*. His most recent historical work is the history of *Eugene's Civic Stadium, From Muddy*

215

Football Games to Professional Baseball. Research from that work provided information for this latest novel, *Crisis In Greenville*, a baseball story about a threatened stadium and a team of rejects.

Other works by Joe R. Blakely include: *The Bellfountain Giant Killers*, *The Tall Firs*, and *A Tribute to McArthur Court*.

Mr. Blakely credits his writing success to Mark Highberger, publisher and editor of Bear Creek Press, William Sullivan, noted Oregon author, and to Dan and Barbara Gleason of CraneDance Publications.

For autographed copies of his books contact Joe Blakely at 541-688-4643, email him at: josephb@uoregon.edu or write to P.O. Box 51561, Eugene, Oregon 97405-0910.

www.ingramcontent.com/pod-product-compliance
Lightning Source LLC
Chambersburg PA
CBHW071005280626
47160CB00015B/1395